POISON PEN

JACQUELIN THOMAS

Poison Pen © 2018 by Jacquelin Thomas

ISBN: 978-0-578-40951-1 (Print)

Cover Design: Rebecca Pau (The Final Wrap)

Prologue

The October weather was cool, and the wind was howling, the eerie sound bouncing off the tombstones, some centuries old, and others like the one nearby, erected a few days ago.

All around, fearless magnolia trees stood sentry over the graves as the wind whistled through fresh cut grass.

Across the grounds a stream of cars including a black hearse were parked at the curb, while black-clad mourners sat beneath a tent to say final goodbyes. Some of them could be heard crying while one after the other laid flowers atop the coffin.

The headstone closest to them felt cold to the touch.

"I never thought we would end up here in such a cold, dark place."

"This is all your fault. You just had to seek revenge. Why couldn't you just do the right thing for once?"

"I couldn't let her win."

"Look around you. We're in a cemetery. You call this *winning?*"

"What did you expect me to do?"

"To become a better person. After everything that's happened, you haven't learned anything. Now it's too late."

"What do you mean that it's too late?"

Chapter 1

June 2008

"Babe, it's just a book signing. It's not like you gonna meet the president."

Bailey Hargrove sent a sharp look toward her boyfriend. "Colton, I'm about to meet my favorite author—the woman whose books have gotten me through the best and worst of times. I have all of her books and this is the first opportunity I've ever had to actually be in the same room with her."

She eyed her reflection in the mirror. The black pants and top in hot pink complimented her deep caramel skin tone and her figure. She wasn't overly dressed up, but professional enough. Bailey wanted to make a good first impression.

Seated on a corner of the bed, Colton chuckled. "You know you sound like a groupie."

Running her hand down the front of her slacks, she said, "I'm just a huge fan of her work."

He downed the last of his bottled water. "Well, I hope she appreciates your support."

"I emailed Harini last week and told her about my book.

She asked me to bring a copy of my synopsis. *Harini Samuels* actually wants to read my work. This is super huge…"

Colton inclined his head, asking, "What's so special about her?"

"Her books are riveting," Bailey responded. She glanced at the clock on her nightstand. Her co-worker and friend, Cassidy would be arriving shortly to pick her up. Bailey pointed to a book on the nightstand. "That's her last book."

He picked it up and stared at the photograph on the back. "Isn't she local?"

Bailey nodded. "Yes, she lives here in Philadelphia. When I was transferred here, I felt like it was confirmation that Harini and I would connect."

Colton put the book back on the nightstand. "And here I was thinking you moved to Philly to be closer to me."

Bailey smiled at her boyfriend of four and a half years. "Colton, you know I love you and I hated the long-distance thing."

Her phone vibrated.

"Oh… Cassidy and Maurie are downstairs." She planted a kiss on Colton's lips. "You going home?"

"I'll probably hang out here until you get back."

"I'll see you later then."

"Have fun."

"I'm super excited." Bailey dashed out of her apartment, taking the elevator to the lobby area.

She walked outside. The afternoon sun baked the city street, softening the asphalt surface making Bailey's every step an effort. The heat wave bounced wildly off the flat concrete walls of the high-rises and beat against Bailey's face like the licking flame of an open fire. She could feel the perspiration spring out like a flood all over her body just walking from her building to her friend's car.

"I feel like I should've brought a change of clothes," she

said from the backseat. "I thought it got hot in Raleigh, but this heat up here is just as bad."

Cassidy laughed. "Just wait until it gets cold. You'll be wishing for summer."

"I don't know about that."

"Why are you so dressed up?" Maurie asked. "It's just a book signing."

"I want to make a good first impression," Bailey responded. "I have my business cards and a copy of my synopsis per Harini's request."

Since graduating from college and leaving North Carolina four months ago, Bailey's life was in an upward swing. Her first manuscript nearly finished, she felt one step closer to her lifelong dream of becoming a published author.

"I'M SO sick of being on display for a bunch of people I care nothing about," Harini complained while slipping on her Louboutin's. "Pip, you know I detest these things. Everybody wants to talk and take pictures with you... all I want to do is sign my books and go home."

"You should be more grateful. You write books... you do book signings. There are thousands of writers who would do just about anything to be in your shoes. New York Times... USA Today bestselling author... you're where you want to be. If you have to engage and smile for the camera—do it graciously. Without your readers—you don't have a career."

Harini nodded, then took a sip of water. "Don't get me wrong, I love the perks... luxury hotels, great food, car service, but you know I don't like people. I can only tolerate them for short periods of time. Some chick already reached out to me about writing. I can't believe I told her to bring me a copy of her synopsis—I guess she caught me in a good mood. I hope this one knows how to use spell check."

Pip chuckled.

"I wonder if a certain author has the nerve to show up tonight," Harini said. "She threatened to whip my butt the next time she saw me."

"Maybe if you stayed out of her business, Joyce Baines wouldn't make such threats. I don't know why you engage in such high school antics, and on social media no less."

"She's the one who's upset. I only spoke the truth and it wasn't like I mentioned her by name. I simply posted that authors need to be careful when they're on tour with other authors. Word gets around about what and who you're doing," Harini said, smiling at her brother. "Rumors are swirling that she slept with an author who is married, then the very next night, she had sex with a different author. That's just messy."

"It's her business, sis. It doesn't have anything to do with you. Besides, it's all gossip."

"Oh, it's true," Harini said. "One of the guys took pictures and I have copies. He told me that she couldn't get enough. He said she was a sex addict."

"I don't want to hear this," Pip responded. "I don't care what other people do—has nothing to do with me."

"You know I didn't start this war. Joyce never should've contacted me about a stupid title. She actually tried to say I heard her talking about it and that I stole it."

"*Didn't you?*"

She glared at her brother. "She doesn't own it. You can't copyright a title or none of us would have any."

"Why can't you just be the bigger person for once?"

Harini mentally ordered herself to remain calm, despite the agitation she felt. "I'm a great person, Pip. All I'm trying to do is help others be successful, but they are just so petty and jealous." Harini believed the best way to avoid being hurt, one had to hit first.

She had never been one to back down from a fight and she wouldn't start now.

"If you're as *great* as you think you are—why can't you keep any friends? Every six months or so, you have a new best friend."

"*Whatever...*" Harini rose to her feet. "I guess I need to finish getting ready for this signing. You staying here or coming with me?"

"I might pop in for a bit."

"If not, I'll see you when I get back."

"Remember these are your adoring fans. Be nice."

"Yeah... yeah..." Harini picked up her purse and checked her appearance in the full-length mirror before heading out. She learned a long time ago that to matter, she had to be the best. Being second best was not an option.

BAILEY and her friends arrived early enough to grab seats on the second row.

"This is so cool," she said, her eyes bouncing around the bookstore, landing on corner and end displays of bestselling books, the in-house coffee shop, reading chairs and couches. "Harini must be so excited about her signing. I know I'd be."

"I imagine it must get old at some point," Cassidy responded. "And exhausting."

"I don't think I'd ever get tired of meeting my readers."

"I was talking more about the traveling. A different city each day." Cassidy placed a hand on her stomach. "I'm tired just thinking about it."

"Feeling nauseated?" Maurie asked.

"A little." She pulled out a tiny pack of saltine crackers. "After I eat these, it should ease off."

Maurie handed Cassidy a bottle of water from her purse. "That's what I dread about getting pregnant—having morning sickness."

"Are you and Lucas thinking about starting a family?" Bailey asked.

"We are," Maurie said with a nod. "We've been married for a year. We're ready to become parents."

Bailey glanced around. All the chairs were filled, and people were lining up in the aisles. "Standing room only. I'm glad we got here early."

Cassidy agreed. "There's no way I could stand through this signing."

Bailey loved the smell of books and coffee. She used to spend hours in a store similar to this one, reading while sipping a cup of coffee or hot chocolate back home in Raleigh, N.C. She would sink into an empty chair as she paged through a book. Caught up in the memory, Bailey ran her fingers over the raised bumps on the cover of Harini's new release.

It was time for the event to begin.

A sudden murmur of excitement rippled through the bookstore behind them. Several splashes of light came down the room from fans taking photographs. Bailey didn't have to turn around to know Harini had made her grand entrance. The sound of whispers plotted that better than radar.

Harini passed her row. Bailey couldn't help but notice the certain free stride in the way she walked. She wore a black tailored suit with a bright, yellow scarf hanging from her shoulders. Her natural hair was a honey blond color and piled high on her head in an explosion of curls.

After a brief introduction, Harini walked up to the podium.

"Thank you all for coming," she said. "What a great way to

spend the evening, huh... surrounded by books, the tantalizing aroma of fresh brewed coffee and the thrill of finding that next great read."

The audience exploded in applause.

Harini's smile was brilliant. "This is my favorite thing to do," she said. "Meeting my readers, so I can't say thank you enough. Please know that I appreciate you all."

Bailey stared into Harini's hazel brown eyes. There was a teasing laughter in them. Her lips parted in a smile as she breathed out the words, "I'm really excited about this story. I had so much fun writing it. This is the fifth book in the Secrets and Lies series. I hope you'll enjoy Meghan's journey into the shark-infested waters of dating and finding Mr. Right. Although for her—it's probably just Mr. Right Now." She chuckled. "I'm pretty sure we can all relate to her at some point in our lives."

Harini read a passage from the book, then answered questions from the audience.

Bailey tapped her foot softly while waiting for the moment she would be able to talk with her favorite author.

She was one of the first ones in line to get her book autographed. Slowly Bailey moved up the aisle, patiently waiting her turn.

Finally.

Harini showed even, brilliant white teeth when she smiled. "Hello. Thank you for coming."

"Hey," Bailey greeted in return. "I'm so excited to meet you. I'm the person who contacted you and you asked me to bring my synopsis."

Harini's brows rose in surprise. "You're not quite what I expected, but it's nice to be able to put a name to a face. So, you're working on a novel?"

Bailey wasn't sure how to feel about her comment but chose not to be offended. "Yes, I am. It's almost done." She was acutely aware that Harini could sometimes be abrasive in her tone, but she didn't get that vibe from her.

"Congratulations," Harini said.

"I'm hoping to submit my book to publishers within the next month or two, so any advice you have, would be greatly appreciated, Miss Samuels."

"There's no need to be so formal. You can call me Harini. Where is your synopsis?"

Bailey pulled it out of her tote and handed the paper to her.

Harini autographed her book, then said, "I'll be in touch."

"Thank you," Bailey murmured. "Oh, do you mind if I take a picture with you?"

"Not at all."

Mindful of the others waiting in line, Bailey had Maurie take a quick photo of her and Harini.

"Thank you again," she told Harini and moved out of the way.

She'd read posts by other writers praising the bestselling author for mentoring them—Bailey hoped and prayed to join this elite group. Having someone like Harini mentor her would be a dream come true.

Chapter 2

After the signing, Bailey and her friends walked over to the deli across the street from the bookstore.

"I'm starving," Cassidy said. "I've been craving a cheesesteak all day, so that's what I'm getting."

Maurie and Bailey decided they would have the same.

"I've only been to a couple of signings back home, but they don't compare to this one." Bailey laid down her menu. "I'm so excited over meeting Harini. I could sit at her feet and listen to her talk all day long." She took a sip of her water. "I can imagine how cool it must be meeting your fans."

"Are you finished with your book?" Cassidy asked.

"The first draft is done," Bailey responded. "I'm in the rewriting stage."

Maurie wiped her mouth on her napkin. "You're the first writer I've met—you know, someone who isn't already published."

"I'm really enjoying this journey. For as long as I can remember, it's all I've ever wanted to do. The only reason I didn't pursue it sooner is because my parents said I needed to get a real job."

"That's what I always thought," Cassidy said, "Writing should be considered a hobby. Not something you do to make any real money. You know, the whole starving artist thing."

Bailey settled back in the booth. "Harini's done well, don't you think?"

"There are a lot of authors out there struggling though. She's just one of a small percentage of authors who is actually making a living off writing."

"Cass, don't be so negative."

She looked at the person sitting opposite her. "I'm not trying to be, Maurie. I have faith in Bailey and the little bit I've read of her manuscript is really good."

"I'm not worried," Bailey said. "I have faith in myself as a writer."

They finished eating and left the restaurant.

Bailey stared out the passenger side window of Cassidy's car during the drive to her apartment located in North Philly.

They turned on her street nearly twenty minutes later.

The tenement buildings were all alike on this block—they had all seen better days.

One day I'm going to live in a beautifully decorated penthouse apartment. I'll have someone to open the door for me… maybe even a chef. I just need to sell my book. I know this is the one.

"What are you thinking about?" Cassidy asked, cutting into Bailey's thoughts.

"How my life will change when my book is published."

"It's a good story," she said, "but do you really believe it's gonna make the bestsellers list? I mean… you're going to be a brand-new author. Nobody will know who you are."

Bailey grinned. "They will after they read my book, Cass. Besides Harini did well with her first book."

"That's because it got the attention of talk show host, Virginia Meadows. She got a lucky break."

"Bailey's got that mustard seed faith," Maurie interjected. "Girl, I'm believing with you."

Cassidy parked in front of the building.

"Thanks for the ride," Bailey said. "I can't believe I actually talked to Harini Samuels."

"Alright fangirl." Cassidy chuckled. "I'll see you bright and early tomorrow morning."

Maurie waved. "Talk to you later."

Bailey got out of the car, wrinkling up her nose. "You'd think the landlord would have the brains to cover the trash can in this heat." She sniffed the air. "It stinks."

There was an uncovered garbage can near the entrance of the building. A filthy looking gray and white cat jumped up onto it and began to rummage through it.

She started up the steps.

A wolf whistle came from across the street.

"I can't wait to move out of this neighborhood," she uttered without sparing a glance at her offender. She moved to Philadelphia right after graduating from college. She was offered a position with Staten Insurance Company after interning with the North Carolina office.

She could hear the shrill wail of a baby as she entered the downstairs hall and began to climb the stairs. The cries grew louder as Bailey neared her door.

She hesitated a moment before opening it.

The baby's screams tore at her ears. She stepped into the room quickly and closed the door behind her.

"So how did it go?" Colton inquired when she entered the apartment. "Did you get to meet the great lady?"

"I did," Bailey confirmed. "Honey, she was so nice... I couldn't believe how sweet she was to me. Harini told me that she'd been in touch. I'm really hoping that she'll become my mentor." Bailey kissed Colton on the lips. "I have a really good feeling about this."

"We should celebrate."

"I was just thinking the same thing," she murmured.

The baby began to cry again, the sound penetrating through the walls.

Annoyed, Bailey uttered, "I need to find another place to live. That's why I really need to sell this book."

"You think you're going to get rich off your writing? You've heard of starving artists, right?"

"Colton, you sound like Cassidy. I'm not just depending on my writing. I'm also trying to move into commercial claims. I'll make more money—enough to get another apartment. A much nicer one."

"You don't have to wait. We can move into a place together."

"We've already talked about this," Bailey stated. "You know I'm not going to live with you until I have a wedding ring on my finger."

Colton flashed her a quick smile that momentarily alleviated the tense lines around his mouth. "One day I'm going to change your mind."

"No, you won't." Bailey kicked off her shoes, picked them up and strolled to her bedroom.

He followed close behind.

"I have to go into the office early," she said.

"Is that your way of telling me you want me to leave?"

Bailey broke into a grin. "I'm saying that I'm not staying up late, Colton."

He laughed. "Actually, I have a meeting in the morning, so I'm not staying here tonight. I'll tell you a bedtime story, then head to my place."

"Bedtime story?"

"Yeah. The one about the beautiful young woman who keeps refusing to take the next step with her one true love."

Bailey eyed him. "Are you talking about marriage?"

"At some point," Colton responded. "Right now, I'm not where I want to be financially."

With a need to escape further conversation on that topic, Bailey said, "We can skip that story tonight. C'mon, I'll walk you to the door."

"You still want to go to Fairmount Park on Saturday?" Colton asked. "I'm asking because my boss wants me to work. It's not mandatory though."

"Good because I really want to go to the park and just hang out," Bailey responded.

"Then that's what we'll do." He kissed her. "I'll give you a call tomorrow. If you're not working late, maybe we can grab some dinner before I head out to Norrisville. I'll be there for training on Thursday and Friday."

"Love you," Bailey told him before locking the door.

She went straight to her room and readied for bed.

Her thoughts landed on Colton. He was the first man she'd ever loved, but she was not going to cohabitate with him. Maybe it was her Christian upbringing or witnessing what her sister went through after moving in with her boyfriend—Bailey wasn't sure which, but she vowed that she would never live with a man without benefit of marriage. She had to admit that there were times when she felt like giving in to him.

Colton's broad chest was fully muscled, and his abdomen was a perfect six-pack. His long legs were sturdy and masculine in shape and the sight of him momentarily halted Bailey's ability to breathe whenever she was around him. A man who looked this good often made it difficult when it came to refusing Colton anything.

Sexy chocolate.

A smile tugged at her lips when her cell phone rang.

Bailey answered, saying, "Look at you... missing me already?"

He chuckled. "I bet you miss me, too."

Colton was right. Bailey loved spending time with him. He wasn't just her boyfriend—they were also friends.

When the time was right, she believed they would get married. Colton was the one man for her; perfect in every way.

"THERE WAS a large crowd at the signing," Harini stated. "That's good, don't you think, Pip?"

"It was standing room only. Always a good thing."

She smiled. "You came?"

"I was there."

"Did you see the way that one girl was gushing all over me?" Tickled, Harini picked up her wine glass. "I think her name was Haley... no Bailey. That was it. You should've heard her gushing all over me with that deep Southern twang. It was so cute. She reminded me of sweet tea, collard greens, and fried cornbread. You know... the way Mother used to cook it."

"She acted like you were a goddess," Pip responded, his eyes twinkling in amusement.

"I *am* a goddess."

"Yeah, I know you really believe that."

Ignoring his sarcastic comment, Harini went on to say, "I think I should get to know this chick. There's something about her that I like."

"She probably reminds you of yourself," Pip said. "She has that same look of hunger that you used to have in your eyes. Her friends on the other hand, wasn't feeling you at all. One of them didn't even bother to buy your book."

"Like I care," Harini muttered. "They don't add value to my life, so they're useless individuals." She refilled her wine glass. "You see that whore Joyce didn't show up at the signing. I knew she wouldn't. She did block me on social media though."

"You need to stop antagonizing folk," Pip advised. "One day it's seriously gonna to backfire on you."

"Do I look worried?" Harini turned on her computer monitor. "Mother used to always say that knowledge is power. She's right."

"What are you about to do?"

"I'm gonna see what dirt I can find on Bailey Hargrove."

Pip shook his head. "You just can't help yourself... can you?"

"If I'm going to work with her—I need to know exactly *who* I'm working with," Harini responded. "In this business, you can't be too careful."

"I guess I'll leave you to your evil doings."

Feeling overheated, Harini gasped in shock. "I can't believe you just said that to me." She unbuttoned the top two shirt buttons. "You need to take that back."

Pip didn't bother to respond.

Harini opened up a window on her monitor, keyed in her user name and password. She waited patiently for the background screening application to load. In order to stay at the top of the publishing game, Harini believed she had to learn as much as possible about her competition—it gave her leverage.

Bailey was not a threat, but Harini found herself wanting to know more about her.

"So, did you find anything juicy about Miss Hargrove?" Pip asked when Harini entered the kitchen later that night.

"No, just that she's an insurance claims adjuster. Looks like she graduated college last month. She doesn't have a huge social media presence... she's basically a nobody—for the most part, Bailey appears to be a pretty decent person."

"How disappointing that must be for you," Pip muttered.

Harini glared at her brother. "What exactly do you mean by that?"

Pip headed toward the door. "I'm going to bed. I'll see you in the morning."

"I love you, big brother, but you can be so irritating at times."

"Trust me… the feeling's mutual."

Harini grabbed a bottle of water from the refrigerator and went upstairs to her bedroom.

She slipped into a pair of pajamas, then climbed into bed with her iPad. Harini wanted to see how many photos from the book signing had been posted. *I took enough of them.* She would post the ones on her phone in the morning.

Harini returned to Bailey's social media page, scanning through post after post.

"She doesn't mention much about her personal life," Harini whispered to the empty room. "This just means I'll have to find another way to learn her secrets."

———

THE NEXT DAY, Pip surveyed Harini's trash can, which by the volume of paper stashed inside, indicated a solid effort. "It can be slow at times," he said. "Don't let the lack of progress deter you, sis. Maybe approaching what you do have from a different point of view is the way to go."

"I was actually considering exactly that." Harini offered a tight-lipped smile. "You know plotting isn't a strength for me."

He laughed. "Now that's funny. Plotting is all you ever do."

"Don't you have something to do?"

"The only reason I'm here is because of you," Pip responded dryly. "I can always leave."

"I'm sorry for snapping. I'm tired and trying to get this book ready for my agent… it's just not coming together."

An hour later, Harini still hadn't made much progress with her writing. She sighed in frustration.

She spent the next hour on the Internet, checking to see if there were any new photographs posted of the signing or if readers were talking about her new book. There were a couple of reviews already posted, but Harini wasn't satisfied. *There should be more reviews by now. I need people to post.*

The truth was that only her first two books had done well —so well that she made USA Today and New York Times bestselling lists. The other two books had not performed as well, so Harini needed high sales on this new release. "I can't fail at this," she whispered. "I can't…"

She was overwhelmed.

Harini closed her eyes, inhaled deeply, then exhaled. She was twenty-six years old with five books under her belt. Her first two books had been optioned for film adaptations. *I've done well. Better than a lot of authors out there, but I have to stay on top.*

She thought about going to Pip but changed her mind. Harini rose to her feet and walked over to the window in her office. She stared out. *I can do this. I just need a short break. I'm putting too much pressure on myself.*

Harini returned to her desk and sat down.

She opened her tote and retrieved a copy of the synopsis Bailey had given her. Harini began to read.

Although there were still a few gaps in the story, Bailey had a strong outline. Harini imagined the manuscript to be a well written one. She had potential—there was no denying that.

She's not as good as me though.

Harini put away the synopsis and went upstairs.

Upon entering her bedroom, a wave of loneliness washed over her. It was a longing so intense, it manifested itself as a dull ache. Her last relationship had ended a couple of months ago, and Harini was currently in between friends. She had her brother but… Hugging herself, she shook away the thought.

A thickness in Harini's throat, signaled the onset of tears. Outside of being a bestselling author, she yearned desperately to be a mother. She'd lost three babies over the past five years and deemed it unfair that she'd been denied the chance for motherhood. Her hand clenched into fists as anger coursed through her veins.

God, I've never asked you for much. I would've been a great mother. Harini raised her eyes heavenward. *You let people who are undeserving have children, but not me. Why? Why can't I be a mother?*

Out of pure boredom, Harini sat down to watch a movie, then took a shower.

After slipping into a pair of pajamas, she made her way to the kitchen.

"I'm about to make a sandwich," Harini said when Pip appeared. "I'm hungry." It would've come as a surprise if he hadn't popped in—it was his way. He often seemed to appear out of nowhere, startling her. Maybe it was because they lived in a 3000 square foot condo. Harini hadn't gotten used to having so much space. Although she grew up in a nice home, it didn't compare to what she had now.

"Did you get any writing done?" he asked.

"Nope. I watched a movie instead." Harini retrieved a packet of deli meat, Swiss cheese, mayonnaise, and mustard from the refrigerator. "I just couldn't focus."

"Why do you think that is?"

"I don't know," Harini responded as she put together a turkey and Swiss sandwich.

"Every writer goes through a period where the story just isn't coming together. It's just a temporary setback. I'm not worried about it."

"I hear what you're saying to me, but the expression on your face tells me something different," Pip stated.

"You'd like that, wouldn't you," Harini snapped, slamming the cabinet door. "You would love to see me fail. You're just like mother and father."

"If you really think that, then why am I here?" Pip questioned.

"*Why are you here?*"

"I hate talking to you when you get like this. I'm out."

"Pip… I'm sorry."

Her words were met with silence.

"Come back please. I don't want to be alone."

Chapter 3

On Saturday, Colton ended up having to go into work, much to Bailey's disappointment, so she spent her morning at the gym working out.

An hour later, she returned home, showered and completed two loads of laundry. Her apartment was small, so it didn't take long to clean.

Shortly after two in the afternoon, Bailey was going stir crazy, so she decided to go out for lunch. She left her apartment and headed down to the corner deli.

"*Bailey…*" A girl's voice behind her called.

She turned and looked back.

It was her neighbor. She waited for the girl to catch up. "Hey Sherrie."

She was out of breath from hurrying up the block. Sherrie was a tall, full-figured girl of twenty-three. She was a year older than Bailey and had thick curly hair and dark brown eyes. "Where are you going?"

"Just walking down to the deli. I'm in the mood for a tuna hoagie."

Her friend fell into step with Bailey. "Sounds good. I think I'll join you?"

A half-smile crossed her face. "You were already headed there. Weren't you?"

"You caught me," Sherrie responded with a chuckle. "Girl, the diet thing just wasn't working out for me. Those expensive meals didn't do nothing but tease me. I was hungry all the time. I think I'll try becoming a vegetarian. Cut out all meat. But first I'ma get this ham and cheese hoagie. I'll start my new way of life next week."

Bailey laughed. "Why don't you come workout with me at the gym?"

"Girl, you know I'm allergic to exercise. Just thinking about it breaks me out."

"You missed the book signing. Harini was great. I'm starting her new book tonight."

"I had to work a double shift," Sherrie responded. "I ordered a copy of the book online. It should be delivered on Monday."

"I would've gotten you an autographed copy."

Sherrie shook her head no. "Not at full price... no thank you. I'm not paying twenty-four dollars for a book, especially when the last book wasn't that great."

Bailey's brows rose in surprise. "You didn't like it?"

"It wasn't good to me," Sherrie glanced over at Bailey. "C'mon... You read it, didn't you?"

"I did."

"So, what do you think about it?"

"I agree that it wasn't her best work, but I enjoyed the story."

After ordering their sandwiches, Sherrie said, "Let's take them back to my place."

"Sure, but first, I have to get my water ice."

"Girl, you have to say *wudder* ice. Then it sounds like you from Philly."

Bailey chuckled. "You always teasing me about the way I talk. I'm Southern and I'm proud of my accent."

Chuckling, Sherrie said, "I like your lil' twang."

After spending another hour with her neighbor, Bailey settled down at her place to work on her manuscript for the rest of the afternoon.

Three hours later, she decided and take a break to check her email. Bailey gasped in surprise when she saw a message from Harini.

Bailey:

    Ms. Samuels wanted to let you know that it was a pleasure to meet you the other night at her signing. In fact, she would like to finish the conversation you two started regarding your writing career. Per her instructions, I am extending an invitation to you to join Ms. Samuels for lunch on Wednesday, June 18th at one o'clock p.m. Please reply with your response and I'll forward the address.

    Best Regards,

    Pip

    Assistant to Harini Samuels.

Colton arrived around seven-thirty p.m. to find Bailey bursting with excitement. She was eager to share her news.

"You're not going to believe this, Colton. I just got an email from Harini's assistant. She's invited me to lunch at her home." Bailey talked fast as she often did whenever she was excited about something. "I've got to find the perfect outfit to wear...I wonder if I should take my laptop or the manuscript...I—"

He chuckled. "Babe, slow down."

"I'm sorry. I'm just so excited. She invited me to her *home*. Not a restaurant. This is so cool."

"Wow, you must have really made a great first impression."

"I hope so." She took his hand and led him to the walk-in closet in her bedroom.

"What should I wear?"

He gave a short laugh. "You've got nothing but clothes. I'm sure you'll be able to find something cute. You look good in everything, babe."

"Colton, I really need your help," she said from within the closet. "I want to impress Harini."

"I think you've already done that. She *did* invite you to lunch. We have to celebrate. If I can get you to come out of that closet, I'll take you to dinner."

She peeked out. "Pita Chip?"

He grinned. "If that's where you want to go."

"I just need to change and then I'll be ready." Bailey quickly slipped out of the shorts into a pair of jeans.

She walked out of the closet, then checked her reflection in the full-length mirror.

At the restaurant, Bailey and Colton both selected the Chicken Shawarma rice bowl.

"I really need someone like Harini in my corner. I'm nervous about this meeting."

"Babe, relax... she reached out to you for a reason. You have a great story so stop stressing."

"You really think so, Colton?"

Colton lifted his drink in a salute. "I do. You're a good writer."

Bailey reached across the table, taking his hand in her own. "I really appreciate your support. You believed in me when my own family basically laughed at the idea."

"When you get that publishing contract, we'll see who's laughing then."

"I just want you to know this means a lot to me, Colton." She finished off her food.

"Thanks for saying that, babe. Hey... sorry about this

afternoon. If you want, we can go to Fairmount Park tomorrow after church. I was thinking we could have a picnic…"

Bailey smiled. "Sounds perfect to me."

The idea of taking a stroll or going horseback riding, then enjoying a relaxing and romantic picnic was exhilarating. The last time Bailey was there was with Maurie and Cassidy. They had taken her on a Victorian-style trolley to tour the Colonial-era mansions dotted along the landscape.

"It's a date," she said, running her fingers through her short curls. Bailey lifted her chin. Staring intensely at Colton, she asked, "What are you thinking right now?"

He broke into a grin. "I'm actually thinking about how sexy you look. Your hair, your eyes, the curve of your hips and the way those hips sway invitingly when you're walking. Bailey, everything about you screams sexy."

She looked up into his eyes, saw them spark and flash and knew she loved him deeply. "I never thought I'd meet someone like you," Bailey said. "To be honest, when we first met—I believed you were putting on an act to impress me. Here we are four and a half years later and you're still the same man I met in Hornsby Hall."

"I've watched you grow, Bailey… into a beautiful and confident woman. Don't get me wrong—you were cute in that freshman way, but you've evolved into straight gorgeous."

She laughed. "You're so good for my ego. I guess that's why I'm crazy about you."

"I feel the same way," Colton said. "I don't think I can face a future without you in it. Bailey, you mean the world to me."

Squeezing his hand, Bailey said, "If things keep going the way they are, we will never have to worry about being apart."

HARINI LIVED in the prestigious Washington Square West neighborhood.

"Oh my goodness… this is so nice," Bailey whispered as she pulled into entrance of Le Maision condominiums. Before she had a chance to cut the engine, the uniformed attendant was holding the door for her. Bailey never received this kind of service before.

"Nice day, Miss. Hargrove," he said, falling into step with her as she walked toward the revolving doors. "Miss Samuels is expecting you."

She stopped and looked at him.

There was a knowing grin on his face.

"I guess this happens all the time."

"Actually, it doesn't," the attendant responded. "Miss Samuels usually does not invite anyone to her home. I've worked here for two years and you're only the third or fourth person I've ever let inside this building as a guest of hers."

Bailey nodded. "Wow…" Hearing this made her feel special.

She stepped into the elevator, quickly noticing that there were no dirty mats on the floor, stale cigarette smoke or a mixture of sweat or body order—all the smells she encountered in the one at her apartment.

Harini was standing at the door waiting for her.

"It's nice seeing you again, Bailey."

Her eyes traveled from her face to the length of her body, prompting Bailey to wonder if she should've worn a suit other than the navy and white sundress. "Thank you for the invitation."

"I have a confession. I'm not much of a cook, so our lunch is catered," Harini said as she led Bailey through the foyer and into the living room.

"I cook, but I can't say that I'm great at it," Bailey responded. "Although I can throw down on some spaghetti."

Harini chuckled. "That's one of my favorites."

"I'll have to make you some," Bailey said with a smile. Her gaze traveled the room. "The food smells delicious."

There were a couple of people dressed in black working in the huge kitchen.

"Bailey... you look a little nervous."

She glanced over at Harini. "I have to confess that I'm a little star struck."

"You needn't be. I'm just a woman who gets to do what I love most—write for a living."

"That's what I want," Bailey said. "To be able to write full-time."

"It's not as glamorous as you may think," Harini said in a loud whisper. "If you want to get where I am—you're gonna have to treat it like a business. It's hard work."

"I'm up to the challenge," Bailey said.

Harini smiled. "I believe you are. You're gonna do well." She rose to her feet graciously. "Lunch is ready to be served."

Bailey followed her to the formal dining room. Observing the eight chairs, she recalled what the attendant about Harini rarely entertaining guests, so why such a large table? She dared not ask. *It's none of my business.*

Harini's next words captured her attention.

"Tell me about yourself, Bailey."

"Well, I'm from North Carolina and I've been up here for a few months." Bailey picked up the napkin and spread it across her lap.

"So, what brought you to Philly? Your job?"

"That and my boyfriend," Bailey responded. "Colton grew up here. He and I have been dating since our freshman year in college."

"How sweet," Harini murmured. "Are there wedding bells in the air?"

Bailey grinned. "Maybe one day, but I'm not in a hurry to walk down the aisle. I really want to focus on my writing."

"One of the reasons I invited you here was to get to know you, Bailey. From the moment we met, I felt that we shared a special connection—like kindred spirits. I see a lot of myself in you."

"Really?"

Harini nodded. "I had that same hunger for the written word—same as you. Writing is my life and I love it."

"So, do I," Bailey said. "It's the first thing on my mind in the morning and the last thing at night. Since working on this book, I've been so focused that I've abandoned my morning devotion. I need to get back on track with spending time with the Lord."

"You're a church girl, huh?"

Bailey laughed. "My father was a pastor. He died last year."

"Oh dear… I'm so sorry for your loss."

"He was a good man. He just spent most of his time at the church which made my mama very unhappy. When my sisters and I left home—we went our separate ways and just never looked back. One sister lives in California. She's married and has two kids. My other sister is in Germany. Her husband is in the Air Force."

"Where's your mother?"

"She's in Kansas City with her sister. My aunt has dementia and my mama takes care of her."

Bailey noticed that Harini didn't offer any personal information about herself. She didn't pry at the risk of offending her. But deep down, she found it ironic that Harini could be so private when she spent so much of her energy exposing the secrets of others on social media platforms.

Every time Bailey saw one of Harini's scathing posts, she asked herself why she wanted to work with a woman who attracted so much drama—the answer was clear. Bailey wanted to become published and she felt building a relationship with Harini would help in her quest. *She had flaws like everybody else. Nobody's perfect and who am I to judge?*

———————

HARINI STRUGGLED to keep her expression blank. Just being in the room with Bailey—she felt her body temperature rise. The girl was oblivious to her beauty and perfectly-shaped body. Her nostrils flared every time Bailey spoke about her writing. Harini wanted to be happy for her, but deep down she couldn't be—there was a chance she could become Harini's competition.

"Come with me," Harini said, "I'll give you a tour of my home. Most people are curious to see how I live. I've been asked by magazine editors if I would allow them to photograph my home. Thus far, I've only let one feature my place. An interior design magazine."

Bailey's gaze bounced around her surroundings. "Your condo is gorgeous. Did you decorate it yourself?"

"I did," Harini responded as they walked down the hall. "This is my sanctuary."

Behind her, she heard Bailey's gasp. Without turning, she knew that the young woman had never in her life seen such a luxurious room. It was a sapphire blue and gray theme for the drapes, the bedspread, even the overstuffed chair near the bed. The carpet was a silver color and the furniture a rich, platinum-tinted wood.

"Wow… this is so beautiful," Bailey murmured.

"Thank you."

Harini led her to a door at the other end of the hallway. "This is my brother's room."

"He's the one who sent me the email."

She gave a slight nod. "Pip's my assistant. He handles my correspondence, social media accounts, my newsletter... stuff like that."

"It's nice that he is so supportive of you."

Harini agreed. "He and I have always been close. He's been with me from the very beginning."

"That's great," Bailey responded. "Do you have any other siblings?"

"No, I don't."

Bailey thought she detected a twinge of sadness in Harini's gaze, but it disappeared as quickly as it had come. She changed the subject by saying, "You have a really nice home."

Harini grinned. "Thanks, hon."

They returned to the living room.

"Have you been looking for an agent?" Harini inquired.

"I haven't," Bailey responded. "It's still a work in progress. I figured it was much too soon to even think about agents."

"I read your outline and I have to say that you did a great job fleshing out your story."

"Thank you," she said. "This means a lot coming from you, Harini."

"I have a great eye for talent. *Real talent.*"

They talked at length about the writing process.

An hour later, Bailey said, "I've taken up enough of your time. Thank you so much for lunch and everything."

"You're welcome," Harini stated. "We'll have to do it again."

Bailey stood up and grabbed her purse. "I'd like that."

Harini walked her to the door. "My doorman will see to it that you get home."

"I drove my car."

Admiring the ring on her finger, Harini said, "I haven't driven in almost five years. I guess I was thinking that less people are driving now that we have other options."

Bailey smiled. "It's cheaper for me to just put gas in my car and go."

She left and drove home.

It was depressing to walk into her dreary little apartment after spending a few hours at Harini's condo. Bailey glanced around and released a long sigh.

Voices from next door grew louder. Her neighbors were fighting again. Soon, the baby would start crying.

As if on cue, Bailey heard a loud wail.

"I'll be so glad when I can afford a much nicer place," she whispered. "I've got to get my book published. All my hopes and dreams are pinned on this book."

Chapter 4

Thin spaghetti straps exposed Bailey's shoulders, the silk material hugged her curves and the plunging neckline provided a provocative glimpse of her neck, even-toned skin and cleavage. She ran her fingers through her short dark hair.

Colton was due to arrive at any moment for date night. They decided to order take-out and enjoy a quiet evening at her apartment. Bailey wasn't in the mood to go out after such a long day at work.

A few minutes after eight o'clock, the doorbell rang.

"You look beautiful," Colton said when she opened the door. "I thought we were staying in tonight."

Bailey grinned. "We are." She hugged him. "I'm so glad you're here." Noting the expression on his face, she said, "Don't go there with the whole I can be here all the time."

"What are we doing?" Colton asked as they settled down to watch television in the living room.

She looked over at him, confused. "What are you talking about?"

"Bailey, why won't you let me move in here with you? We love each other. What's the problem?"

She released a long sigh. "You know, I haven't heard you mention anything about an engagement ring or better yet… marriage, Colton."

"So, we have to be engaged?"

"No," Bailey responded, "We would have to be married."

"Are you *serious* right now?" Colton wanted to know. "I know you a PK but that's like on some real old-fashioned level. We've been together for almost five years."

"I'm fine with the way things are between us," Bailey stated. "You're the one who wants to just cohabitate. I'd rather have marriage and I'm not going to compromise on that."

"You know you're the only woman for me, Bailey. You know we belong together."

"Knowing all that isn't going to change my mind, so you'd better renew your lease or find another apartment."

"Maybe you don't love me as much as you say," Colton muttered, his gaze pleading.

"That's not going to work with me," Bailey responded with a chuckle.

"I can't believe you're being so stubborn about this. Think about the amount of money we could save if we live together."

"You just refuse to give up."

Desperation seemed to fuel his words. "Babe, we can get engaged if that's what you want."

"Colton, I need you to really listen to me. I'm not trying to manipulate you into anything," Bailey stated. "I'm just not going to live with you or any other man before marriage."

Colton sighed in resignation. "I don't like it, but I'll respect your decision."

Bailey could tell he wasn't happy, but she had to stick to her guns.

The movie started, putting a stop to the discussion of living together.

When it ended, Bailey noticed that Colton wasn't as talkative as he normally was.

He's upset with me.

"Colton, I love you," she said.

He nodded. "I know that. I just don't think you should let your parents influence your decisions."

"My dad raised his children in the same way that he led his church. He gives us what the Bible says. It's up to us to follow the laws of the Lord." Bailey met his gaze when he glanced over at her. "If I allowed my father to rule over me, you and I wouldn't be sleeping together."

Colton smiled. "Lucky me."

Bailey cut her eyes at him. "Don't sound so happy about it."

"You talk about wanting to quit your job and write full-time. We could save your income by living together."

"You said there's something going on with your company," she pointed out. "You may not have a job much longer."

"I'm just trying to be supportive, Bailey. If you're home, you will have more time to write."

"I appreciate your wanting to do this for me, but Colton... we have to be practical. You know how much I love you, but we're ever going to agree on this topic. I want a husband one day—not a live-in boyfriend."

"OH, I know she not trying to send me a subliminal message," Harini blurted. "Pip... come here..."

"What's happened now?"

Startled, Harini uttered, "I wish you'd stop sneaking up on me like that!"

"Why are you always so jumpy?"

"I'm just upset. Kaile Jefferson clearly don't know who she

messing with... all the stuff I know about her... I know all about her foreclosure and bankruptcy. Instead of trying to attack me on the sly—she needs to take a class on money management."

"What did your former best friend say?"

"She's been making comments about authors who criticize other's literary work. Kaile seems to think that authors who do this are petty and jealous."

"And you really think that she's talking about you?" Pip asked. "Not everything is about you."

"I *know* she is. She and I had words last month over some feedback I gave her on that disgrace of a novel. I told her the truth. It's not my fault she couldn't handle it. I was merely trying to keep her from becoming an embarrassment."

"Telling Kaile that her book sucked wasn't exactly the right way to get your point across, sis. You wouldn't leave it there. You had to send her a price list for your writing workshops. You were supposed to be her friend, sis."

"I'm not one for sugarcoating my words—never have been. As for the classes, she'd be a much better writer if she took some of my workshops. I *know* how to write," Harini said. "Matter of fact, I'm one of the best writers I know. That's why so many authors come to me for help. They just have to understand that you can't have thin skin in this business. It's better for me to tell them that their book is horrible than to have readers posting one-star reviews."

Harini eyed the computer screen. "I got something for Kaile though," she uttered. "I heard she paid somebody else to write that book for her—that's why she struggled so much with the revisions."

"Do you really want to co-sign on a rumor?" Pip asked. "One that you have no proof of being true."

Harini ignored her brother while her fingers flew over the keyboard.

"Did you hear me?"

"Too late. It's out there."

People want to call themselves a writer, but instead of putting pen to paper—they hire someone else to do the work. That's fine if a person wants to do that, but at least find someone who can ACTUALLY write. Remember, you get what you pay for.

"Was that really necessary?" Pip asked.

"Well, it's true," Harini said. "If you gonna pay someone to write a book for you, find someone who knows how to *write*."

"You do know that you can be sued for slander."

"It's not slander if it's true, Pip."

"You don't know that?"

"I do because the person who did the job told me. She also told me that she had to threaten to put Kaile on blast just to get all her money. She sent me a screenshot of their agreement."

"You know what this really is about. You're just mad that Kaile didn't ask you to ghostwrite the book."

"She would've had a bestseller if I'd done it."

"And she'd be paying you half of her royalties in addition to your standard fee."

Harini nodded in agreement. "Of course. I don't come cheap."

"You're headed down the wrong path, sis."

"I know what I'm doing."

"Keep telling yourself that. The truth is that you don't know how to be a real friend."

"I have a meeting with Edna tomorrow," Harini announced, abruptly changing the subject. "She's coming to Philly."

Surprise registered on Pip's face. "Your agent is coming to town?"

Harini nodded. "That's what she said. She wants to have lunch. I have a feeling that it's going to be about my sales. I've already contacted a marketing specialist for some advice."

He scanned her face. "You look worried."

"I'm not," Harini said. "My new book seems to be doing pretty well. I am gonna ask Edna why there is only six cities on my tour. They shortened it this year."

"Likely because of your numbers on the last two books."

He was telling her something she already knew. "I'm gonna get something to eat." Harini picked up a menu. "I'm in the mood for Thai food. What about you?"

Her brother shrugged in nonchalance. "Sure. That's fine."

Harini hadn't been completely honest with Pip. Deep down, she was worried about this meeting with Edna. The only time her agent wanted to meet in person was to deliver news about her sales or to request major revisions to a proposal. Harini didn't care for either topic because it implied that she had failed in some way. If her mother were still alive, Harini could hear her complaining about her imperfections; and bemoaning her embarrassment and humiliation.

I'd like to see her sit down and write a book. It wasn't as easy as everyone thought.

Harini couldn't understand why she could never please her parents. Nothing she ever did brought a smile to her parent's faces. She was never good enough.

She shook the painful thoughts from her mind. Harini didn't want to think about such sad things right now. She needed to prepare mentally for the meeting with Edna. She had to convince her agent that she could still deliver a best-selling novel.

Harini stared at what she'd written on the computer—it was good, but it could be so much better. *I know I can do this. I just need to get out of my own head. I'm overthinking it.*

Her stomach protested, reminding her that she never

ordered dinner. Harini ordered the pineapple duck entrée from Xiandu. "Thank God for online ordering," she whispered, rising to her feet.

She left her office.

"Pip, I'm going to pick up dinner. You want to ride with me?" Harini asked, forcing a calm demeanor.

"I'll be here when you get back," he responded.

Harini picked up her purse and keys. "Okay then."

She bit down on her bottom lip, but not enough to draw blood. Harini was not looking forward to her meeting with Edna.

Downstairs, she waited for the attendants to bring her car to the front entrance.

Nervously, Harini paced the marble floor.

Her apprehension increased during the eight-minute drive to the restaurant. "This is ridiculous," she told herself. "I don't have anything to worry about. Everything is gonna be fine. I can handle Edna."

THE MOMENT ARRIVED.

Harini strolled into the Rittenhouse Hotel and headed straight to the Lacroix restaurant inside. She loved the charm and rich history of the luxury hotel in Center City. After her first book made USA Today, Harini spent a weekend in one of the well-appointed rooms, wanting to experience the fine dining and invigorating spa treatments.

"Hello Edna…" she greeted before taking a seat at the table. Harini did a quick assessment of the expensive suit her agent wore. *She's able to afford clothes like that because of me.*

"It's good to see you, Harini. I know you're leaving town tomorrow for your tour, but I wanted to see you before you left." Edna brushed away a long blond curling tendril.

"I appreciate you coming to see me off like this."

A waiter walked up to take their drink orders.

"Sales have been down for your last two books," Edna stated when he left the table.

"Well, Mrs. Ex just came out." Harini took a long sip of water. "I'm feeling pretty good about it. It's the forth book in the series."

"Presales weren't where they usually are," Edna picked up her menu. "I think it's time to let that series come to an end. I met with your editor last week. Snyder and James want to see something new from you."

Harini frowned. "I still have at least two more books for this series."

Edna shook her head. "They want new material, Harini."

She leaned forward, saying, "I've made Snyder and James a lot of money."

"Not with the last two books."

"Mrs. Ex will make up for that." Harini folded her arms over her nervous stomach.

Edna didn't seem as confident. "I hope so."

"I can't believe this," Harini uttered while trying to contain her frustration. "I've written five books for them—all of them have been on a bestsellers list. I've been nominated four times for the Global Literary Award and won twice. Yet Snyder and James are ready to kick me to the curb because of low sales on the last two books." She glared at Edna. "You're supposed to have my back. Snyder and James haven't done all they could do on their end, and don't forget I told them that cover on the last book was going to hurt sales. *I was right.*"

"This is why I'm here, Harini. Why we're having this conversation."

"I have to tell you that I'm not feeling appreciated."

"Snyder and James are still behind you, but you know how this works, Harini. It's about the numbers."

"Sales are down all around, Edna. You know this…"

The waiter returned with pen and paper in hand.

"I'll have the Maine lobster roll," Harini said, although she didn't have much of an appetite.

"The turkey club," Edna interjected.

While waiting for their food to arrive, Harini eyed her agent. "So, if I want another contract, I'm going to have to come up with something new, something fresh."

"Yes," Edna stated.

She sighed. "I really don't like feeling pressured. It doesn't help my creativity."

"You're a prolific author, Harini. I have every confidence that you'll be able to come up with a new story—something fresh. One that your readers will love."

When the waiter returned with their entrees, Harini forced down her meal and struggled to remain pleasant, although she was disappointed with Edna.

The woman was supposed to have her back. She was supposed to fight for her. Harini felt betrayed. She silently debated whether or not it was time to shop for a new representation.

"How did it go with Edna?" Pip asked when Harini stormed into the house, flinging her purse on the sofa.

"Not well at all." Biting her bottom lip, Harini sank down on the soft, buttery leather sofa. "I'm so angry right now, I could spit blood."

"What happened?"

"She told me that the publisher wants me to come up with new material. They want Mrs. Ex to be the last book in the series."

"I take it that you don't like this idea."

"You know how hard it is for me to come up with solid storylines, Pip. I can't deal with this right now. And Edna… instead of fighting for me, she's agreeing with them."

"Your sales have gone down."

"You think I don't know…" Harini snapped. "I heard this all afternoon from Edna."

"Sis, she's on your side. Don't forget that."

"Is she really?"

"You're upset right now."

"That's an understatement," Harini muttered. "I need a glass of wine."

"It's not a bad thing."

"I don't want to talk about this anymore, Pip. It's giving me a headache." Harini rose to her feet and made her way to the kitchen where she poured herself a glass of white wine.

I just can't believe this. Nobody has any loyalty anymore.

Harini sipped her wine slowly as she worked to relax her body. She'd been tense all day.

What I need is a nice massage.

She made a mental note to schedule an appointment with her favorite spa.

Harini remained in a funk for the rest of the afternoon. The fact that she didn't have a man in her life only added to her frustration. She didn't even have a friend she could call to vent.

Life just wasn't fair.

Chapter 5

Bailey drew her finger along the rim of her navy and white coffee mug as she fantasized how her meeting with Harini later that evening would go. If God decided to answer her fervent prayer, she would soon join the ranks of published authors. She had faith that it was her calling.

Her eyes traveled the length of the crowded cafeteria. Bailey enjoyed her job, but working claims was not something she wanted to do until she reached retirement age. She was born to be a writer.

Outside the building, the wind shrieked, and rain poured. In weather like this, accidents happened, and claims were higher than normal.

"Girl, I just got off the phone with a customer," Cassidy said, taking a seat across from Bailey. "She never read her policy, so she didn't know that she didn't have rental and a high deductible. She was yelling at me like it was my fault. I had to conference her agent in because she thought I was lying to her."

"I had one of those calls earlier," Bailey responded. "I can't wait to get this day over with. I'm meeting with Harini on Monday."

"When did that happen?"

"She called me just before I left to come in here." Bailey glanced over at the giant chalkboard sign filled with menu items that hung on the wall behind the counter. "I think I'm going to have the fish and chips."

"Me, too," Cassidy responded.

They rose to their feet and got in line to order their food.

Bailey eyed the soft sage-colored walls, the bright lighting a warm, flattering shade of gold.

"Did Colton propose or something?" Cassidy asked. "You been walking around grinning all day."

After they had gotten their food and returned to the table, Cassidy said, "I hope you don't get mad at me for saying this, but Bailey… I'm just not sure about Harini. There's something about her I don't trust."

"You don't know her."

"No, I don't," Cassidy agreed, "but I watched her at the book signing and I'm sorry, all that stuff she was doing and saying; it was just an act. She's *fake*. I used to follow her on social media and she's a trip."

"She was a little over the top, but maybe this is how she engages her readers. And you're right. She can be a bit controversial, but the woman knows how to write." Bailey smiled. "Besides, I like people who have no problem telling it like it is."

"I'm all for being honest, but I don't agree with character assassinations and public humiliation. This is what she does to anyone who doesn't agree with her or confronts her about something. She sets out to destroy them."

"Cass, what's your problem?" Bailey questioned. "Why do you have to be so negative? This is an opportunity to help get my own book published. If connecting with Harini is the way to do that, then I'm going to take a chance with her."

"She's an Internet bully."

"But you have to admit that she isn't always the one starting the drama. Harini just doesn't back down."

"But why does it have to play out for the world to see? I just don't like stuff like that."

"Neither do I," Bailey confessed. "But I'm not going to judge her. Is that why you didn't buy a copy of her book? Because she starts drama."

"I didn't buy one because I don't care for them. You love her writing, but I don't. I only went to the signing to hang out with you and Maurie."

Bailey wiped her mouth on her napkin. "She's been nothing but nice to me, Cass."

She did not respond.

"I have a really good feeling about this," Bailey said. It was okay that Cass didn't like Harini—she was mature enough to understand that there were some in her social circle whose personalities might not mesh well. It had nothing to do with her.

"Okay," Cassidy responded. "If you have peace about it, then go with it. Just make sure that you're not blinded by the fact that you want this so badly."

Later that evening, Bailey gave Maurie a recap of her conversation with Cassidy.

"I'm afraid I have to agree with Cass. Harini can be the queen of petty. You need to be careful who you align yourself with."

"I'm smart enough to stay away from the drama. I'm just focused on getting my book published, and Harini can help me with that."

"Be careful of what you tell her," Maurie warned. "'Cause if you piss her off, she just might use the information against you."

"I'm not stupid," Bailey said. "Besides I don't have any

scandalous secrets hidden away. I don't have anything for Harini to hold over my head."

"I'M HAVING dinner with Bailey tonight," Harini announced. "I'm meeting her at The Fountain, although I'd rather be dining at LaCroix, however, I'm sure Bailey can't afford the appetizers much less a main entrée."

"When did you become such a snob? I remember when eating at McDonalds was a treat."

"Those days are long gone, Pip," she said, her mouth tightened.

"Sis, you need to rethink this," he stated. "I know what you're planning."

"It's not a big deal. I'm just gonna be her mentor," Harini responded, "and why shouldn't I? She looks up to me like a loyal subject. I'm the queen of African American Fiction."

"Sis come down off that pedestal. Let's keep it real. Bailey simply respects the woman you portray. You and I both know who you really are, *Harini*."

She glared at him. "I'm so tired of people judging me. Mother and Father judged me... these nobodies try and now you..."

"Then stop what you're doing," Pip said. "Stop looking for dirt on other authors; stop writing nasty reviews on books you haven't even read... just *stop*. It's like you get off on shaming folk. It's not right."

"I do try to read those books—they're just not well written. I've studied my craft for years and I'm still working hard to perfect it. I just ordered a new set of writing reference books this morning."

"Yet, you can't write a story from start to finish without help."

Her brother's words stung. "I can't believe you just said that to me."

"I did," Pip responded. "I will always tell you the truth. Most of your problem is that you're very insecure when it comes to your writing. You want to be the best at everything—number 1. When are you going to get it that none of that stuff matters."

"It never mattered to you," Harini snapped. "Everything has always come easy for the *golden child*. Our parents thought you could do no wrong."

"And this is where it got me."

Silence.

"Pip…"

"You should get back to work," he said, "you need to get something to your agent."

Folding her arms across her chest, Harini said, "I know you think I'm a horrible person, but I'm not."

"I never said that. You just make terrible choices."

She picked up her purse. "I have to go."

Ten minutes to seven Harini walked The Fountain. She had arrived early and was seated immediately.

Bailey arrived at seven p.m. sharp.

At least she's prompt, Harini thought to herself. That's good. Being late was a pet peeve of hers. She didn't like to be kept waiting. This time she wore a chic sapphire blue suit with a black silk camisole and heels.

Harini's nostrils flared when she realized that every single male in the restaurant seemed fixated on Bailey as she approached the table. *She's cute but I'm better looking. I have so much more to offer a man than she does.*

Bailey sat down in the chair opposite Harini. "Have you been waiting long?"

"You're just in time," she responded.

While they waited for their drinks to arrive, she noted how

Bailey's head was slightly bent as she listened intently whenever she was speaking. It thrilled Harini to have Bailey's complete attention. "I remember so well what it was like to be waiting for that first chance of getting published. It was so nerve-wrecking."

"Yes, it is," Bailey admitted. "I'm almost done with my final revisions. I've worked on this book for almost a year. I really believe in my story."

"You're on the right track," Harini told her. "You have a great work ethic. I'm the exact same way."

"How hard was it for you to get published?"

"Actually, it was pretty easy. I sold the first book I wrote."

"That's wonderful." Bailey wanted the same to happen for her. She wanted this first book to sell and top the bestseller lists. She'd dreamed it, believed it and thought it possible. Maurie often teased her about having mustard seed faith—well, she did.

They continued to talk about the literary world while they ate.

When they finished their meals, Harini signaled for the check.

Their waiter edged toward them, then paused at the table beside them before presenting her with a black leather folio.

The woman seated across from them threw down a black American Express card, then removed a small gold compact from her oversized Chanel tote and began inspecting her flawless image.

"That's Michele Allen," Bailey said in a low whisper. "I *loved* her in Winter Island Heist. She is an incredible actress."

Pressing her lips flat, Harini gave a slight shrug. "She was alright."

When Bailey continued to gawk at the actress, Harini's irritation increased. "Clearly, you would rather be having dinner with her."

"Oh no… I'm sorry. It's just that I don't get to see a lot of celebrities."

"Then maybe you should join the pack of paparazzi waiting for her exit." Harini glimpsed the hurt expression on Bailey's face and softened her tone. "They're just people like you and me. If I'm going to be your mentor, I can't have you walking around all star-struck."

Bailey gasped. "Are you for real right now?"

"Yes."

"Harini, thank you so much."

"You're welcome. You should know that I don't take just anyone under my wing, Bailey. You're a very lucky girl."

At home, Harini gave her brother a recap of the meeting. "Pip, I thought the girl was going to lose her mind over seeing Michele Allen. That overactor."

"Bailey was excited about meeting you as well. What's the problem?"

"I just don't see what all the hype's about with that actress. Her skills are seriously limited as far as I'm concerned."

"Why are you doing this?" Pip asked. "You can't stand working with other authors."

"Bailey's different."

"You mean she's naïve. She actually believes that you care about her."

Harini sighed in frustration. "I *do* care about Bailey."

Pip grunted in response.

It bothered Harini that her brother had no faith in her; much like her parents. She would show them. She would show them all.

BAILEY AND COLTON met for lunch the next day.

"Harini's going to be my mentor," Bailey announced after they were seated in a booth.

"Congratulations, baby."

"This is like a dream come true for me." She picked up her menu. "But honey, you won't believe who was sitting at the table next to us—*Michele Allen.*"

"For real?"

Bailey nodded. "She was there. , Harini acted kind of funky with me because I was excited about seeing Michele. She actually got an attitude about it."

Colton laughed. "She wanted all the attention on her. You sure you wanna work with someone like that?"

Bailey laid down her menu. "We were having a business meeting. I should've been more professional, I guess. That's probably why she was tripping like that, but the evening wasn't a bust. She did offer to mentor me."

"Wouldn't it be better for you to just get an agent?" Colton asked. "What can Harini really do for you? It's not like she's a shortcut to getting published."

"I'm not looking for any shortcuts," Bailey sniped. "It's always nice to get feedback or advice from someone who's already made it to where you want to go. My company has a mentorship program. So, does yours."

"Calm down, babe. You don't have to act so defensive."

Bailey met his gaze. "I don't like what you were implying. I worked hard on my book and I will do whatever I have to do to get it published. I don't want Harini to walk it to her editor or anything like that. I'm a hands-on learner."

"I know you work hard at everything you do," Colton responded. He reached across the table and took her hand. "I have faith in you, babe."

"I'm not one of those people who are looking for someone to give me anything. I've earned everything I've ever gotten. My getting published will be no different."

Chapter 6

On Friday evening, Bailey shared her news with Cassidy and Maurie while having dinner at their favorite Italian restaurant.

"That's wonderful," Maurie said while Cassidy remained silent.

"I'm pretty excited about it," Bailey told them.

"Cass, you haven't said anything," Maurie commented. "This is a great opportunity."

"I'm sorry. I just have a bad feeling about it."

"She thinks Harini is fake," Bailey explained. "It's okay. We don't have to like the same people and I really appreciate Cass's honesty."

"Don't get me wrong," Cassidy said. "I want you to achieve your dream of becoming a published author. I really hope she's sincere about mentoring you."

Maurie held up her wine glass. "So, let's toast to dreams coming true."

"Yeah," murmured Cassidy. "Dreams coming true."

"Amen to that," Bailey added. "May all our dreams become our reality."

"So, how are things between you and Colton?" Maurie inquired while slicing into her Chicken Marsala.

"He's still trying to convince me that we should live together."

"You and Colton love each other, and you've been together for what? Four years?" Cassidy inquired. "He wants to share living space with you. Why do you keep turning him down?"

"It's not something I believe in," Bailey responded. "I want to have a nice wedding… the works. I feel like if Colton and I live together—we'll end up in nothing more than a common law type of situation. I'm not going to settle." Bailey stuck a forkful of shrimp and fettuccini drenched in a scampi Alfredo sauce into her mouth.

Maurie nodded in agreement. "I see your point."

"Has Colton mentioned marriage at all?"

Bailey eyed Cassidy. "He says it's the plan, but that he's just not ready yet. He wants to be more financially sound first."

"So, basically he wants all that comes with marriage except the piece of paper."

"That's what it sounds like to me," Maurie interjected.

Bailey nodded. "That's how I feel about it. Cass, I know you and Joe lived together, but you were engaged to him."

"Yeah. When I found out I was pregnant, we went ahead and had a civil ceremony. We're going to have our wedding after I have the baby as planned. We're married already—I don't need anything else, but Joe wants to have a big fancy wedding. He wants it because it would make his mother happy."

"When I get married, I just want something small and inti-mate," Bailey said.

They trio took in a movie afterward.

It was a little past midnight when Bailey walked into her apartment. She showered, changed into pajamas and climbed into bed.

She hadn't heard from Harini since the night they had dinner. Bailey didn't want to be a pest, so she didn't call or text her.

It was fine, she decided. Bailey intended to spend her time finishing up her book—the same way she started—on her own.

"I KNOW you've been working really hard on your book for the past couple of days, so I brought ice cream. You need to take a short break and just relax." Colton shook the white bag as proof. "Your favorite. Lemon raspberry white chocolate."

He waited until Bailey finished her typing before handing it to her.

"You are such a sweetie," she said, opening her treat. "I've given myself a deadline and I intend to make it."

"There's a spoon in the bag."

"You've thought of everything." She pushed away from her desk and stood up. "You didn't get any ice cream for you? You know I don't like to share."

Colton broke into a grin. "I'm watching my physique."

They navigated to the table in the small dining area.

Bailey sat down across from him. "How was your day?"

"Just okay," he responded. "I've been telling you that something's going on at work. I'm pretty sure that it's time to update my resume. There's been rumors circulating that there are going to be layoffs."

"Again?"

Colton nodded. "I survived the last one, but I don't know about this time. We have an owner, so I'm sure he's bringing some of his own people." Leaning back in his chair, he inquired, "How's the writing coming along?"

"It's going great. Harini gave me some really good feedback." She dug into the carton, pressing hard to fill her spoon. "I'm so lucky to have her in my life."

"I was thinking we could go to the Poconos next weekend."

"Colton, I can't," Bailey said. "Harini and I are going to a writer's retreat in Maryland. She just told me about it earlier today."

"Oh," Colton said. "Have fun."

"I know we were planning to spend the weekend together, but I really don't want to miss this opportunity. All the authors I've read will be there." Bailey broke into a grin. "I get to learn from some of the best."

"We'll have other weekends."

"Colton, you're not disappointed, are you?"

"A little," he confessed. "I was looking forward to getting away, but I know how important this is to you."

"I promise I'll make it up to you." Bailey pushed away from the desk. "I appreciate you for giving me space so that I can focus on my writing. I love you so much."

He kissed her. "I love you too, babe. More than you could ever imagine."

"You know… I think I'm going to call it a night… with the writing, I mean."

Colton grinned. "Really?"

Bailey nodded. "Yes. Why don't we finish this in the bedroom?"

BAILEY CHECKED into her hotel room.

Harini had flown down to Baltimore earlier that day, but Bailey decided it was more cost effective for her to drive. Colton rode down with her.

She'd dropped him off at the house of a friend of his from college.

She punched a contact in her phone. "Hey Harini... I just checked into the hotel. I'm in room 228."

"I'm in 440. Give me about ten minutes and meet me downstairs at the registration desk."

"Okay," Bailey said with a smile. This was her first writers retreat and she was beyond excited. There were several workshops she wanted to attend. She noted the times and location in her planner.

When it was time to head down, Bailey left the room and took the elevator to the lobby area.

She found Harini surrounded by a group of writers. Smiling, Bailey walked over to join them."

Harini introduced her. "This is one of my mentees. Bailey Hargrove. Remember that name."

She stood by silently while Harini answered questions and talked up her writing classes. "They are hosted online for six weeks... if you want the tools to writing a bestselling book, then you definitely need to take my class."

Bailey wondered why Harini had never once mentioned her writing classes to her.

Maybe she thinks I don't need them. Regardless, Bailey decided not to make a big deal of it.

"Let's get our badges."

She followed Harini to the registration area.

"Have you been to this retreat in the past?" Bailey inquired.

"I've come every year since its inception. I teach a class on characterization and one on writing description."

She pulled out a copy of the program agenda. "I've already made a schedule of the classes I want to attend this weekend."

"The only ones you need to take are *mine*," Harini stated. "They are the best ones here at this retreat."

"I saw that Kaile Jefferson has one on plotting. I thought it might be interesting."

"Humph...."

Bailey eyed Harini. "You don't think I should take it?"

She shrugged in nonchalance. "It's up to you. I'm here to teach my workshops, then spend the rest of my time at the pool or in the spa."

Bailey a little put off by Harini's attitude. But then she was already a veteran writer—it's not like Harini needed to take workshops on a craft she had already perfected.

After picking up swag bags, Harini decided she'd had enough of being around the attendees. Bailey opted to stay downstairs and network.

"Didn't I just see you with Harini Samuels?" a woman wearing a name tag that read Sharon Colby.

"Yes," Bailey responded.

"She's one of my favorite authors."

Bailey smiled as the woman prattled on and on about Harini. *Is this what I sounded like*, she thought.

She released a soft sigh of relief when they were joined by another attendee. Bailey chose this moment to make her escape. "I need to check in with my job. I'll see y'all later at the reception."

In her room, Bailey laid down across her bed, her mood buoyant. She could hardly wait for the festivities to begin.

FOR THE WELCOME RECEPTION, Harini chose a pale pink Chanel suit with a cream-colored, lacy blouse underneath, and nude Louboutin heels that clicked on the highly polished marble floor of the hotel lobby.

"Well, look who's here."

At the sound of a disturbingly familiar voice behind Harini, there went her mood for the rest of the day, right into the toilet. She arranged her smile before turning. "Hello, Kaile. What are you doing here?"

"It's a writer's retreat. Why wouldn't I be here, Harini? I've been coming to this retreat nearly as long as you have."

"I figured you'd given up writing, or did you come with your ghostwriter? Make sure the two of you take advantage of some of the workshops." Lowering her voice, Harini added, "You both need them."

Anger flashed in her eyes. "What you need to do is stop going around here spouting those lies? I saw what you posted on social media. I don't and have never had anybody write a book for me."

"Kaile…" Harini broke into a chuckle. "If you use one, it's not a big deal. Just find one who can actually write and keep her mouth shut."

"You are such a spiteful woman," Kaile hissed. "Morgan and I are cowriting a book, Harini. What you probably read was a rough draft of our project, although I can't imagine how you got your hands on it."

"Well, I certainly hope it a first draft. It wasn't any good. F.Y. I. your girl has a big mouth. *She's* the one telling all of your business."

"That would sting if I actually cared what you thought, Harini." Lowering her voice, she said, "I'm also tired of you making comments about me being broke. You don't know what you're talking about."

"Bankruptcies are public record."

"Yeah, I filed years ago, but I didn't have to go through with it, Harini. The man I'm dating—he's paid off all my debt and he bought me a new house. A beautiful 4500 square foot house. No mortgage as in *I own it*. Now run tell that."

Harini forced a smile. "Well, I'm glad you don't have to live in the streets."

"You're a piece of work."

"And you wish you were the writer I am. Kaile, I can see it written all over your face. You will never be as good as me."

Kaile sighed. "That's the thing, Harini. I'm not in competition with you. I've never been. You want to be number one—to be the best. I just want to write my stories and get paid. I hope all your success keeps you warm at night."

She walked away before Harini could think of a suitable response.

Yeah. Her mood was definitely in the toilet.

Flush.

Chapter 7

Bailey wore a pair of black jeans, white, silk tee shirt underneath a red blazer. Although she considered herself fashionably chic, she felt underdressed beside Harini.

Seated at their table, Bailey observed her mentor stroll around the ballroom as if she owned the place. Harini's very presence commanded notice.

Cass was right about her, she decided. Harini did put on an act whenever she was around a lot of people. She personally didn't have a problem with it, although Bailey could never see herself doing it. She wanted her readers to get to know the real her—not some made-up persona.

"Would you mind getting me a white wine?" Harini asked when she joined her at the table.

Bailey's eyes landed on the bar located a few feet away from where they were seated. "I don't mind at all," she said, rising to her feet. The only reason Bailey was doing Harini's bidding was because she was in the mood for a glass of wine as well.

"I hope you're not becoming Harini's little errand girl," said a voice said from behind her.

Bailey turned around to face Kaile Jefferson. "Oh hey."

"Just an FYI. She's going to ask you to get her food. Take my advice and tell her to get it herself."

"Excuse me…"

"You seem like a really nice person," Kaile said. "I've been in this industry for several years now—long enough to know who to stay away from. Harini is one of those people. Be careful around her. She's not your friend."

Bailey met Kaile's gaze but did not respond.

"Just be careful." She gave her a tiny smile before walking away.

"What did Kaile have to say?" Harini asked when Bailey returned to the table with two glasses of wine. "I saw her talking to you."

Bailey sat down. "She introduced herself. That's pretty much it."

"She's a very envious person. Not someone you want to be around—unless you like drama."

"I like my life drama free," Bailey stated. Although she kept her thoughts silent, Harini also carried a lot of drama with her as well. A lot of the attendees seemed to avoid being around her.

Harini seemed not to notice, but Bailey caught her unguarded reactions from time to time. It was during moments like this that her mood swings took over. Bailey simply chose not to be offended by Harini's snide remarks or curt responses.

"Oh, they just put out some crab cakes. Be a dear and get me some."

"I'm… I need to go to the bathroom." Bailey walked briskly out of the ballroom. She was not about to spend her weekend being Harini's personal server.

When Bailey returned to the table, Harini was holding court with another attendee as she munched on crab cakes, meatballs and chicken drumettes.

She ignored Bailey.

That's fine with me. I'm not her slave and I'm not going to kiss her behind.

Bailey got up and navigated the room, meeting some of the other attendees. When she returned to the table, she was surprised to find a plate of desserts waiting for her.

"I remember you telling me how much you love chocolate, Bailey. It's also my weakness, so I thought we'd indulge together."

Bailey broke into a grin. "Thank you, Harini. Chocolate is a weakness of mine for sure."

"Well, I'm declaring this a guilt-free weekend for us both."

"I'll get us a couple of glasses of red wine to go with all this decadence," Bailey said. "We might as well live it up."

"Ah yes… red wine and chocolate. A girl after my own heart."

From across the room, Kaile's gaze was on Bailey, who summoned a smile. Whatever was going on between her and Harini had nothing to do with her. She was not taking sides or participating in their drama.

Later that evening, Bailey sat in her room wondering if she'd made the right decision in choosing Harini as her mentor. The woman had an ego the size of the building; she was selfish and petty; believed others should serve her, but then there was the other side of her. The one who helped other writers with learning their craft; she could be thoughtful at times. Even when she refused to get food for her, Harini had made sure to bring her a plate of dessert.

Realization dawned on her. Harini had done that bit of kindness to make a point. Bailey burst into laughter. "She's so petty."

"HOW WAS YOUR EVENT?" Colton asked when she picked him up Sunday afternoon.

"Interesting," Bailey responded. "The workshops were great. I learned a lot that I'll be able to apply to my manuscript."

"That's good. Did you meet any of your other favorite authors?"

"I did," she responded. "I met Kaile Jefferson. She told me that I need to stay away from Harini. It's pretty clear that they don't like each other. I must say that it's a bit disappointing that there is so much drama in the publishing industry."

"Babe, there's gonna be drama everywhere you go. It's the way of the world."

"Colton, you won't believe this. Harini thought I was going to stand in line, prepare plates and bring them to her. She's not handicapped in any way."

He chuckled. "Yeah, she don't know you. You've never been one to do another person's bidding like that."

"I'm definitely not the one for that," Bailey said. "I'm just going to focus on writing my books. I'm not kissing her behind just so she can mentor me."

"Have you considered that Kaile might be right about Harini? You said she's been writing for a while. She would know."

Bailey dismissed his words with a wave of her hand. "I'm a pretty good judge of character, Colton. I trust my instincts."

HARINI TOSSED the clothing from her suitcase onto the floor. "I saw Kaile sniffing around Bailey at the welcome reception. It doesn't matter though. By the time I'm done with that witch. She will rue the day we ever met. *Trust…*"

"One day, someone is going to come gunning for you, Harini."

Harini rolled her eyes heavenward. "Pip… you're getting on my nerves. You're supposed to be on my side. We're family. Where's the loyalty?"

"You really want to go down that path?"

Harini clenched her fists. "I've always looked out for you…" She shook her head. "You know what… *forget you.*"

"If only you could," Pip responded. "But the truth is that you can't. You can't because you need me."

She knew he was right, so Harini kept her mouth shut for the moment. She hated fighting with Pip.

Alone in her office, Harini turned on her computer.

She opened up her social media page to see if she'd been tagged in any of the posts from the retreat.

There were a few but less than she expected. Her disappointment deepened. She'd taken pictures with practically everybody that was there.

Harini muttered a string of profanity. There were more posts about Kaile than there were of her. Accolades of how sweet and generous she was when it came to sharing information.

I shared nuggets as well. I also told them about my workshops and the price. People only value what they pay for.

Out of curiosity, Harini checked out Bailey's page on a whim. She wasn't looking for anything in particular. Just being nosy.

She eyed a photo of a grinning Bailey with a tall handsome man. *This must be Colton.*

Harini enlarged the photo.

There were many things to be grateful for in life.

Family.

Friends.

Health.

Wealth.

Chocolate.

All good, but none of them came close to the sight of a gorgeous man—the kind of man who made a woman very aware of her female parts. Harini was sure his tall height lined up perfectly with her five-eleven frame. Colton had broad shoulders and a flat stomach framed by a tapered waist. Every cell of her being was focused, like a laser, on his body. It had been a while since she'd met a man sexy enough to make her drool.

On impulse, Harini sent Bailey a text, inviting her and Colton to dinner. *This is a man I'd like to get to know better.*

Much better.

Harini saved the photograph to a folder on her computer.

THE NEXT MORNING, Harini strolled into the kitchen humming.

"What's got you in such a good mood?"

"Good morning, Pip." She opened a cabinet door and retrieved a coffee mug. "I'm having dinner guests tonight. Bailey and her boyfriend Colton."

"Why?" he asked.

"I want to get to know them better."

"Nope. There's more to this. I know how your mind works, my dear sister. You're interested in getting to know the man— not Bailey. What you're planning is wrong on so many levels."

"It's just dinner, Pip. You're overreacting."

Harini made a pot of coffee. "It won't end there, and you know it."

"If what you say is true, then Colton and Bailey are not meant to be together. It's better she finds that out now rather than later."

"You used to have a heart."

"I still have one, Pip. I just want a man who worships me, is great in bed and makes me feel like a goddess. Someone who loves me, for me. Inside and out," Harini said. "It would be nice if he were six foot four, with sexy eyes and a body that would make a nymphomaniac cry."

"There are plenty of single men out there in the world. Why don't you find one of them? You are coveting Bailey's talent and the man she loves."

"Why don't you just disappear?" Harini snapped. "You have always been so self-righteous. I guess that's why our parents loved you more."

"You need to stop with the mommy and daddy issues," Pip stated. "You can't blame them for everything wrong in your life."

"Why can't I? They blamed *me*. You were the golden child —the one who made them proud. No matter what I did—it was never good enough."

"And you know why."

"Get out of my sight," Harini screamed. "I don't want to see your face."

"Lord knows, I don't want to be around you either," Pip responded. "Remember, the only reason I'm even here is because a certain person doesn't want to be alone."

His words left Harini shaken.

With trembling hands, she poured coffee into her mug. *I can't think about my brother right now. I need to find a caterer for tonight. I want a special meal prepared.* She recalled Bailey mentioning how much Colton loved seafood, especially lobster.

By the afternoon, Harini had selected a caterer and decided on a five-course meal. She had a feeling, Colton would be impressed by that while providing him a peek into what he could have with her.

Now she had to decide on something to wear—something elegant and sexy.

Harini wanted tonight to be perfect.

"SO, are you ready to go into the lion's den?" Bailey whispered in Colton's ear. They had just entered the elevator and were en route to Harini's floor.

"This place is *nice*. I don't think I've ever been in something so grand. I don't know anybody who lives like this."

"There are only three condos on each floor," she told him.

"They must have a lot of space."

Bailey nodded. "Wait until you see Harini's condo. It looks like what you'd see in an interior design magazine. She told me that hers has been featured in one." She placed her hand in his. "This is what our lives can look like, Colton. We can have all this, too."

"Oh yeah... this definitely works for me."

The doors opened, and they walked into the hallway.

Bailey paused outside of a door. "You look so handsome. I like this suit on you."

Colton leaned forward and whispered, "Seeing you in this dress, all I can think about is taking it off you."

She grinned. "I need you to get your mind off sex; at least for a little while."

Bailey rang the doorbell.

The door opened, revealing Harini who was dressed in a strapless purple and gold jumpsuit. Her long curly tresses, flat-ironed straight and her makeup perfectly applied with a skilled hand.

I'm glad I had Colton wear a suit. I didn't expect Harini to look so glamorous.

"I'm thrilled you two were able to join me tonight for

dinner," she said, stepping out of the way so they could enter the foyer.

"These are for you," Bailey said, offering her a bouquet of flowers.

"They're beautiful." Harini sniffed them. "How very sweet."

They followed her to the living room. "Have a seat. I'm going to put these in water. There's a tray of appetizers over there on the table."

As soon as Harini left the room, Colton uttered, "Man… this place is *tight*. She gotta be making bank off her books in order to live like this. I see why you want her to be your mentor."

Bailey grinned. "Exactly."

COLTON WAS MUCH MORE handsome in person. His social media photos didn't do him justice at all.

Harini checked her reflection in the mirror in her office. *I look exquisite. No man including Colton will be able to resist me.*

She made her way back to her guests. Clearing her throat, Harini said, "I'm about to have a glass of wine. Will you both join me?"

"Sure," Bailey and Colton said in unison.

They stood up and followed her over to the built-in bar area.

"Will your brother be joining us?" Bailey asked.

Harini shook her head no. "Pip's out of town."

"Oh, I was looking forward to meeting him."

"There will be other times." Harini made brief eye contact with Colton and tossed her hair with the gesture she had mastered over the years. Her hair flipped expertly behind her shoulder, and her earrings dangled.

A crease formed between Colton's eyebrows as he returned her smile with a polite one of his own. Somehow Harini didn't think the movement had the effect she'd hoped for. Most men thought it was sexy—the way she flipped her hair when flat-ironed and curled. Colton didn't seem at all enchanted by it.

She covered her disappointment by saying, "We can go into the dining room. Our dinner is ready."

"You have a chef?" Colton asked.

Harini smiled. "No, they're only the caterers. However, I am thinking seriously about getting one, however. It would definitely be cheaper."

For the first course, they ate crostini with white truffle oil and olive paste. Harini chose the oysters casino for the second course.

"This is amazing," Bailey murmured between bites.

Colton nodded in agreement. "I love oysters."

Mixed greens with fresh tomatoes served with a lemon vinaigrette was served as the third course. Harini could tell that her guests were impressed—it was the reaction she was seeking. She wanted to give Colton a peek into the life he could have with her. He only had to choose her. "We're having baked lobster tails and asparagus with a rice pilaf for the main entrée."

"Oh wow," Colton murmured. "That's my favorite food."

Harini smiled. "I'm so glad." She could feel Bailey's gaze on her and looked directly at her. "You eat lobster too, don't you?"

"I do," Bailey responded. "I have to say you've outdone yourself with this dinner. Everything so far has been delicious."

"I hope you'll still feel the same way by the time we're done with dessert."

Colton chuckled. "This is living."

"I bet dessert is something chocolate," Bailey said.

Harini laughed. "You know me so well. We're having

molten chocolate cakes served with a warm black cherry sauce."

Bailey leaned against Colton. "You're right, babe. This *is* living."

Watching the two of them, Harini had never felt such longing for a man in her life and so envious. Looking at Colton made her feel ravenous; it was a raw hunger gnawing at her belly. And when he smiled… Harini felt it from the top of her head to the tips of her toes, and everywhere else in between.

She wasn't desperate by any means. Harini had dated a few men, but things never worked out because they were intimidated by her success. She could tell that Colton was different though—he was smart and accomplished. With her guidance, he could also become sophisticated.

When Bailey glanced in her direction, Harini dropped her eyes. She didn't want to be caught ogling the man in front of his girlfriend.

Colton sliced off a piece of the lobster tail, twirled it into the melted butter, and then stuck it onto his mouth. A mouth Harini wanted to kiss—wanted to feel sliding all over her skin…

"Harini," Bailey said, cutting into her thoughts.

"Oh, I'm sorry." She cleared her throat. "I was thinking about the current book I'm working on. The ideas, they just never stop coming."

"I have the same problem."

Harini chuckled. "It's a good problem to have."

Her gaze locked with Colton's across the table. Harini noted the brief reaction of shock and pleasure in his eyes before he looked away, focusing his attention on Bailey. However, nothing could shatter the connection that was alive and sizzling between them.

Harini knew that Colton felt it, too. She could see it in his eyes, in the firming of his sexy lips. She could also tell that he was struggling with whatever he was feeling. Harini bit back a satisfied smile.

Bailey and Colton did not stay too much longer after dessert. They both claimed to have to be at work early the next morning.

More like they were in a hurry to get home and into bed, Harini thought jealously.

Enjoy him now because soon he will be mine.

In her office, she slid the pencil across the surface of the desk with a finger. *I could tell that Colton feels this connection that exists between us.*

Harini rocked backward in her desk chair, fantasizing about Colton and the things she wanted to do with him and to him. The ringing phone pierced the silence of her small office like a horn, causing her to jump.

It was Bailey.

"I just wanted to thank you again for such a nice dinner. Colton and I both enjoyed ourselves."

An image of Colton formed in her head. "Trust me... the pleasure was all mine. I enjoyed the company."

After the call ended, Harini searched for Colton on social media and sent him friend requests to each of his accounts.

She was sure he'd accept them—after all, she was Harini Samuels.

Rich, gorgeous and sexy. How could he refuse?

Chapter 8

"Be honest. What did you think of Harini?" Bailey asked Colton when they arrived at her apartment. She sat down on the sofa to remove her shoes.

"She's interesting," he responded.

"In a good way?"

Colton nodded. "One thing for sure. She's high maintenance and has expensive taste. I loved her condo though. That five-course meal... I could get used to dining like this every night."

"I know..." Bailey responded. "This is how national best-selling authors live. Take note."

"Baby, you need to get to your computer," Colton said, "Hurry up and get that book finished."

"I'll get right on that," she responded.

Colton smiled at her, a smile that wove heat through her entire body.

"Actually, let's not worry about the book tonight." Moving closer to him, Bailey said, "You know... I have a better idea."

"What's that?"

She stood on tip toe and whispered in his ear.

"I like the way you think, baby." Colton swooped her up into his arms and carried her to the bedroom. "You are the only woman in the world for me."

COLTON ACCEPTED Harini's friend request. What started off as harmless flirtation ended up with him coming over two weeks later.

Harini's eyes bounced around the living room. The only light emanating from candles, giving the space a romantic glow.

"Project seduction underway…"

Without turning around, she said, "Pip, what are you doing here? I figure you would've disappeared by now, especially when we're not getting along."

"I was hoping that you'd actually come to your senses."

"Stay out of this."

"Why don't you do the same?" he demanded.

She waved her hand in dismissal. "Goodbye, Pip. I'm not doing this with you tonight."

"You really need to listen to me on this. Bailey is not the one to mess with."

"*Goodbye.*"

Pip left in a huff.

Harini took a deep breath and relaxed her shoulders. She wanted to be in a peaceful state of mind. She wanted tonight to be perfect.

Colton arrived promptly at nine o'clock.

She put a smile on her face and opened the door. "It's good to see you." Harini stepped aside to let him enter.

His gaze swept to her eyes and then slid downward, taking in the strapless black dress with the thigh-high split. Colton walked straight into the living room and sat down on the sofa.

She strolled over to where he was sitting. "I'm happy you're here," Harini said as she sat down beside him.

His gaze scanned her face than traveled downward. "You look nice."

A thrill coursed down Harini's spine as Colton held the eye contact for much longer than a brief second. Touching his cheek, she said, "You seem a little nervous."

"All the way over here, I kept asking myself why I was doing this. Coming here," Colton said. "Bailey's a nice girl and I really care about her."

Taking his hand in her own, Harini responded, "Yet, you're attracted to me."

"I won't deny that you're a very beautiful and very sexy woman."

"Just admit it." Harini said. "You are just as curious as I am about where this takes us."

Colton inclined his head. "You're not shy at all."

"I don't have time to play coy," she stated. "I see something I want—I go after it. I've always been this way." Harini looked up at Colton's face, still holding his hand. "Can you handle my truth?"

Colton nodded silently, his eyes on her face.

She stood up.

Harini felt something emanating from him. A kind of weakness. She knew she had Colton when he got up and stepped toward her.

"There's no coming back once we go down this path," she warned.

"I know."

She raised her mouth to his lips.

Colton matched her kiss for kiss.

Harini knew her pull was inexorable and something he could no longer fight. She undid Colton's shirt buttons, her mouth following, gliding over his chest.

He stepped backward. "Heey… not here. Not like this. Your brother's home. He could walk out his room any time."

Harini wriggled her fingers beneath the slope of his belly, reaching for his belt buckle. "You don't have to worry about Pip. He's in his room for the evening."

"I'd feel better if we were in your bedroom," Colton said. "Not here in the open like this."

"How cute," she murmured. "I assure you. My brother won't be disturbing us, but if it will make you feel more comfortable… c'mon let's go to my room."

Once there, Colton took hold of her shoulders, pulled Harini in close and kissed her. For one split second, she thought he'd pull away, but that moment passed in a heartbeat. His tongue tangled with hers, sending streams of pleasure shooting through her, dazzling Harini's brain, enflaming her body.

His hands on her back felt like live wires, searing her bare skin. Lifting one hand, he pushed his fingers through her curly tendrils. "You are a temptation I know I should refuse, but I can't. We shouldn't be doing this."

"Honey, we were meant to do this."

Harini moved into him, leaning closer still, wrapping her arms around his neck. "Make love to me."

After their passions were spent, they lay entwined in damp sheets. Harini snuggled closer to Colton, who jumped up as if he'd been shot.

Without saying a word, he padded across the floor to the bathroom.

Gently biting her lip, Harini shivered. Without Colton's body beside her, she was chillingly aware that she was naked.

Harini pulled the blanket all around her, but it didn't help. She felt an acute sense of abandonment.

He walked out of the bathroom. Colton wouldn't look at her.

Harini broke into a grin. "I'm cold. Why don't you come back to bed?"

"I need to leave," Colton responded without emotion.

She watched him pull his shirt over his head and tuck it into his jeans. Harini reluctantly reached for her robe. "I had a nice time with you, but I have to be honest. I'm feeling like a whore. You might as well leave money on the nightstand."

The room was enveloped in tense silence.

Why is he acting so distant now? Harini wondered. *Was he ashamed of what they'd done? Was he so tied to Bailey that he regretted their lovemaking?*

She couldn't just let him walk out the door without a discussion. "Look, I know that you care about Bailey. That she was your college sweetheart, but you have to consider that maybe you've outgrown her. I can look into your eyes, Colton. I know that you feel something for me, too. Our attraction is mutual."

"I don't deny that I'm attracted to you, Harini. But I can't dismiss that Bailey and I have something good together."

"If that were true, you wouldn't have made love to me the way you did."

"It was just sex, Harini." Colton made his way to the door, shoes in hand. "Let's not try to make it more that it is."

"Colton…"

He turned around to find her standing up stark naked. "Are you sure you want to leave?"

Muttering a curse, Colton dropped his shoes and began removing his shirt.

Harini gave him a triumphant grin.

IT WAS ALMOST noon and Harini had a meeting with Edna. Last week when they'd talked over the phone, she implied that she was working on a new proposal. Her agent was in town to discuss it.

In the middle of her bedroom, Harini swiveled to examine herself from the side view in the full-length mirror on the closet door.

"You look good, sis."

"I ought to look good, for the price this outfit cost." Harini swiveled again and admired the rear view. The cost of the clothing she wore on her body right now could probably buy a villa on a private island somewhere. For this meeting with Edna, Harini had chosen a sharply cut, cream-colored Dolce & Gabbana suit with matching Jimmy Choos.

She grabbed her purse and car keys.

Harini drove to the Rittenhouse Hotel.

Edna was waiting for her in the lobby. "Don't you look divine."

"Thank you," she responded. "I'm loving this black suit you're wearing. It's a Elie

Tahari, right?"

"Yes. You have a great eye for fashion."

They found an empty area where they wouldn't be disturbed and sat down.

"You didn't have to come all this way, Edna. I could've emailed you the proposal."

"I was going to be in town anyway. A friend of mine is getting married this weekend. I'm the maid of honor, so I came in early to help with all the last minute things that have to be done."

"It's not a series proposal as I mentioned on the phone. Right now, I need to stay published and since Snyder and James think I need to go in a different direction—I'm willing to try it with this one book."

"Fair enough," Edna stated.

Harini handed her agent the proposal of her story—the

main concept was adapted from Bailey's synopsis. She'd made some changes to it—the title, the names of the characters... just enough to call it her own.

She took a long sip of water. "I worked really hard on this idea."

Edna grinned. "This is great, Harini. Now, this is what I'm talking about. We're back to classic *Harini Samuels.*"

"I'm glad you like it, but will Snyder and James?"

"They're going to love this proposal, Harini. I have a really good feeling about this. In fact, I'm calling your editor now."

When her agent finished her phone conversation, Harini said, "Sounds like she's interested in seeing my proposal."

Edna smiled. "She's very excited about it. Send me a copy and I'll email it to her today."

Harini pulled out her phone. "I'll email it to you right now."

She spent the next hour at the Rittenhouse Spa and Club. It was the one place Harini felt that she could truly relax.

She and Kaile used to always meet there at least a couple of times a month. Their friendship ended when Harini made disparaging remarks about Kaile's writing skills, although she truly believed that the woman was jealous of her.

As soon as she entered the facility, she was greeted warmly. Harini always requested the same services; the organic sacred facial, the deep moisture wrap, and the sacred nature mani/pedi.

She thought about Bailey.

I did what I had to do. This is my career and it's all I have. Besides, my readers will expect a story like this to come from me—I know exactly how to tell it to make it come alive—to make it shine. It's not like I plagiarized her story. My spin on it is actually a much better one. She could never tell it the way that I can.

Harini knew that Pip would never approve of what she'd

done, but it didn't matter. She had to do whatever possible to save her career.

Anybody would do the same if in her shoes. She just had the guts to admit it. Harini also knew that authors like Kaile were too afraid to take her on—she knew too much about them and would expose their secrets in a heartbeat.

Harini guarded her secrets well. She would never allow someone to have that kind of power over her, which is why she did not seek out friendships. The only people she allowed close to her were those she considered her competition. She firmly believed in keeping her enemies close.

She shared little of her personal life, although others felt compelled to tell her their life stories. Harini didn't understand why people allowed themselves to be bogged down with everyday struggles. She had learned a long time ago—she had to do whatever possible to control her destiny.

Chapter 9

"Colton, did you get my message?" Bailey asked when he answered his phone the next morning. It wasn't like him to not call or text her back.

"I'm sorry, baby. I went out with the boys last night and got in late."

"You must have gotten a little drunk as well," she said, amused. "You didn't respond to my texts or my voicemail."

Silence.

Bailey glanced at the phone in confusion. "Hey… you still there?"

"Yeah, I'm here."

"You okay?" she asked.

"I'm fine," Colton responded. "Hey, can I call you later? I need to jump in the shower. I didn't realize it was this late. I was supposed to be in the office thirty minutes ago."

"Sure. I'll talk to you then."

Bailey ended the call, then walked over to Cassidy's desk. "So, where are we going for lunch?"

"I thought you had a date with Colton."

"I just got off the phone with him and he didn't mention it.

He went out with the boys last night. He sounded like he had a hangover. Anyway, will you be my lunch date?"

Cassidy chuckled. "Of course, I will. You know I'm always down for food."

"Okay, well, I'll see you at noon. I'd better start working my claims before it gets too crazy."

Bailey headed back to her cubicle.

Colton hadn't acted like himself, but she wasn't really worried. He wasn't a big drinker and couldn't handle too much alcohol. He normally didn't drink during the work week. Maybe they were celebrating something special, Bailey considered.

The telephone on her desk began ringing, forcing all thoughts of Colton out of her mind. She needed to focus on her workload.

Right before Bailey left for lunch, Harini called.

"I hope I didn't catch you at a bad time."

"You're fine," she said. "I was about to have lunch with a friend of mine. What's up?"

"I wanted to know how your writing is coming along?"

"It's going well. I should be finished in a couple of weeks."

"Don't rush it," Harini said. "Take your time, Bailey. That's where most writers go wrong—they want to rush the process. Do you have someone to edit your book?"

"No, I hadn't really gotten that far. Do you know of someone?" Bailey chuckled. "Of course, you do. Harini, I don't know why I asked that question."

"I spoke with the young lady I use and she's willing to edit your book. However, she won't be able to get to it for a month."

"That's fine," Bailey responded.

"Great. I'll text her contact information to you."

Bailey was touched. "Thanks Harini. You've been so incredibly helpful. I can't tell you how much I appreciate you."

Cassidy approached her desk just as her conversation ended with Harini. "Was that your new B.F.F.?"

Bailey chuckled. "You're funny."

"C'mon girl… I'm hungry. You know I'm eating for two. I need food."

Picking up her purse, Bailey said, "Let me get you to a restaurant before you run out of fuel. I don't want Joe coming after me if anything happens to you and that baby. Do you know what you want to eat?"

"Wings. I'm in the mood for some hot wings."

"Sounds delicious," Bailey murmured. "I think that's what I want as well."

Lunch over, it was back to the office.

Bailey spent the rest of her day on the telephone, fielding calls from customers. She ended up working an extra hour to keep her claims under control.

Colton called her shortly after she got home from work. Bailey was just about to find something to make for dinner. "You sound a lot better," she told him.

He chuckled. "Rough night."

"I bet."

"Have you eaten?" he asked.

"No, I was just about to try and figure out something."

"How about the pizza place on the corner?" Colton suggested.

"Near my place?"

"Yeah."

"You want to meet me there?" Bailey asked as she headed toward the door. "I can leave now and place the order. It should be ready by the time you get here."

Colton laughed. "Open the door, baby."

She did.

He was standing outside her apartment.

"How long have you been here?"

"From the moment I called you," Colton responded.

Bailey quickly grabbed her purse and keys. "Let's head out."

"Is something bothering you?" she inquired when they were seated at the restaurant. Colton was usually more talkative, but he'd barely said more than two sentences to her during the drive.

"Why do you ask?"

"You're not acting like yourself, Colton. Is there something more going on with your job?"

"Rumors are still circulating, but there's nothing concrete," he responded. "I guess the uncertainty is unsettling."

"You're going to be fine," Bailey assured him. "Any bites from any of the companies you sent your resume?"

"Not yet."

"Do you want to see a movie on Friday?" she asked. "Denzel has a new one coming out."

"I've already made plans with my boys. We can go Saturday night if you want." Colton picked up his menu. "What toppings do you want on your pizza?"

Laughing, Bailey said, "I can't believe that you asked me that. I always get the same thing.

I'm predicable. That's what Cass always says."

"Do you believe that about yourself?" he asked.

Bailey shook her head. "I don't think so. I just like certain foods, but I'm also willing to try new things." She paused a moment, then said, "You know what... Let's get something different. Let's try a veggie pizza."

"Really?"

She broke into a grin. "Yes. We can still get our pepperoni and sausage, but let's order a small spinach and mushroom."

"Cool," Colton murmured.

After placing their order, he reached over and took her by the hand. "You know I love you, right?"

"Of course, I do." Bailey surveyed his face. "What's this about?"

Colton reached into his pocket and pulled out a gift. "This is for you."

She opened it, revealing a black velvet box with a sapphire and diamond tennis bracelet inside. "This is so beautiful..." Bailey glanced up at him. "What did I do to deserve such a nice gift?"

"It's a small token of my love."

Grinning, she asked, "Are you sure this is not a *get out of the dog house* gift?"

Clearing his throat noisily, Colton inquired, "Now why would you say that?"

"Honey, I was teasing."

Bailey noted that Colton still didn't have much to say while they ate. He was not acting his normal self. She was sure that it had to do with work. He was worried but didn't want her to know it.

"Everything's going to work out," she said.

"Huh..."

"With your job. You'll find another one if it comes to that."

Colton smiled. "You have a lot of faith in me."

"It's well deserved." Bailey wiped her mouth on the edge of her napkin. "I know that you really wanted us to live together, but—"

"You were right," Colton interrupted. "The more I thought about it—the more I understand what you've been saying."

She was surprised by his words. "I didn't expect that to come out your mouth. For the past four or five months, you've been trying to convince me to move in with you. Now you've changed your mind?"

"I just think it's best that we wait until we're sure we're ready to get married."

"I agree," Bailey murmured. "I'm fine with that."

They left and went back to her apartment. When Colton didn't park his car, she asked, "You're not staying?"

"Not tonight, babe. I wanted to spend some time with you, but I brought some work home that needs my attention."

"No problem," Bailey responded. "I understand what that feels like. That's why I stayed late today—I wanted to keep my claims under control, although when I walk in tomorrow morning—I'll have even more waiting for me."

Colton kissed her. "Love you, babe."

"I love you, too," Bailey told him.

She showered and was in bed within the hour. Bailey tried not to let Colton's actions bother her. There was something going on with him—something he wasn't sharing with her. Colton was not one to keep secrets from her, so Bailey wasn't really worried. Colton would tell her whatever he was dealing with whenever he was ready.

FRIDAY NIGHT, Harini stepped aside to let Colton enter.

His hand trailed along the cool skin of Harini's arm. "You look like you've been waitin' on me to come home—did you cook dinner?"

She gave a short laugh. "My cooking dinner for you or anybody is a borderline fantasy, honey."

"So, who does the cooking 'round here? Your brother?"

"If Pip doesn't cook, then we order take out," Harini responded.

"Where is Pip? When do I get to meet him?"

Colton was looking at her as if he could see all the way into her soul. As if he knew what was in her heart and was waiting for a confession.

Harini swallowed, then said, "He flew out this morning to Los Angeles. He's spending time with some friends. Since I'm writing on my next book, it's the perfect time for him to vacation."

"How come you don't have any family pictures up? I've never been to a house where there weren't personal photos anywhere."

Harini bit back her irritation. "Why all the questions, Colton?" She knew he was trying to search out that secret place where she stashed all the feelings she was too afraid to deal with.

"I was just curious."

"I moved in here about a year ago, but I still have a lot of unpacking to do." Harini pulled a stack of menus out of the kitchen drawer, then turned to face him. "What would you like to eat?"

"I'm not really hungry," Colton said.

Harini frowned. "I don't like this mood you're in."

"I've been doing a lot of thinking. I need to be honest with Bailey," Colton blurted. "She deserves to know the truth."

"And what's that?" Harini asked. "What is that truth?"

"That I've been seeing you."

"Colton are you sure you want to do that? Break Bailey's heart for what? A couple of nights in my bed. A *fling*."

"What are you saying?"

"We're just having a bit of fun, Colton. There's no need to ruin what you have with Bailey—not right now anyway."

"It's not easy to face her knowing I've been with you. You know, Bailey thinks you're her friend, Harini."

"Sweetie, we can't help who we're attracted to…"

Colton shook his head. "I've never cheated on her until now."

"Maybe you need to consider that Bailey is not your soul-mate as you believed."

"You might be right," he responded, his gaze traveling

from her face to her naked body. "But this is not the way for me to find out. I'm sorry, Harini. I can't do this."

"You mean you won't do it."

"I need to leave."

Harini slipped on her robe. "You're not being held hostage."

"You deserve a man who can love you the way you deserve."

"I know," Harini responded. "I thought that man was you." She paused a moment before saying, "Are you sure you want to leave? Do you really want to deny yourself?" Opening her robe, she murmured, "This is all yours."

Colton's resolve was weakening. Harini could tell from the expression on his face and the lustful gleam in his eyes. She allowed the silken material to slide down her shoulders to a puddle in the floor.

He was hers.

BAILEY GLANCED up at the clock on the wall. It was half pass two in the morning. She stretched and yawned. From the moment she'd left work and walk through the doors of her apartment, she parked herself in front of the television with her laptop to work on her book.

She had just typed *The End* on her manuscript. A feeling of accomplishment washed over her, prompting a satisfied smile.

It was done.

The feedback Harini had given her was a tremendous help. Bailey had reached out to the editor who stated her schedule was full at the moment. Instead of waiting, Bailey decided to polish it to her best ability, then submit to publishers.

If was late, but Bailey wanted to call Colton. She knew he

was most likely asleep, so she decided to hold off until morning.

She glanced at the clock once more.

I have to work in the morning, so I need to get some sleep.

She couldn't wait to tell Harini that she was ready to begin the submission process to find a publisher. Bailey was so excited she could hardly sleep. She had every confidence that her book would sell.

Bailey turned to her left side.

Colton would be just as excited about this phase of her journey as she. Bailey planned to call him first thing in the morning. Then she would call Harini at some point.

Her eyelids grew heavy. Bailey closed her eyes, letting sleep take over.

The alarm went off as it did every week day at six a.m.

She crawled out of bed, showered and dressed for work.

Bailey had a bowl of cereal for breakfast, then drove to the office. As soon as Bailey was settled, she called Colton.

"Good morning," Bailey greeted when he answered his phone.

"Hey baby."

"I'm not going to keep you, but I want you to know that I love you, Colton. I love you and I'm so grateful to have you in my life. You've believed in me from day one, when I told you that I wanted to be a writer. Even when I didn't have my family's support."

"I love you, too."

"I also wanted to tell you that it's done. The manuscript is finally finished and ready to go."

"That's great," Colton said. "Congratulations, baby."

Bailey smiled. "I couldn't have done this without you."

"Yeah, you could have," he responded. "But I appreciate the sentiment."

"What do you think about going away this weekend to celebrate?" Bailey suggested. "We can go to Atlantic City. I've never been there before and always wanted to go."

"Sounds good to me."

"Great. I'll make the reservations," Bailey said. "Then I'll give Harini a call, so I can tell her the good news."

"Why don't you hold off on telling her," Colton uttered. "Let's just keep this between the two of us for now."

Bailey frowned in confusion. "Okay..." She had no idea why he wanted to wait, but she decided to oblige him. "I won't say anything."

The discussion turned to their plans for later that evening.

"I have to take care of something first," Colton said. "Then I'll be at your place."

"See you tonight."

"Bailey..."

"Yes," she said.

"I love you."

"I know. Love you too, babe."

"That's what I needed to hear," Colton said. "From the moment I met you—Bailey, I knew you were the one for me."

"Then don't do anything to mess it up," Bailey teased.

"COLTON, I didn't expect to see you tonight," Harini said when she walked out to her car. "I'm on my way to meet a friend for dinner." In truth, she was having dinner alone, but she refused to tell him that.

"I apologize for showing up unannounced, but I really wanted to talk to you."

"I can give you five minutes."

"It won't take that long," Colton stated. "I can't see you anymore, Harini. I can't keep doing this to Bailey. She doesn't deserve to be cheated on."

"So, you're back to that."

Colton met her gaze. "I'm sorry."

Harini took his hand in her own. "I really care for you, Colton. That's the truth."

"Bailey... she really admires and respects you. She loves me. What we doing is wrong."

"Clearly you are not the man for her, Colton. It's that simple. You and I... we belong together. I thought you were beginning to see that."

He shook his head. "Bailey and I have a future together and I don't want to mess that up."

Harini shrugged. "If she's what you want, that's fine. I told you before that I wouldn't hold you hostage."

"You're... you're not going to say anything to her, are you?"

"You look scared." Harini glimpsed a flash of anger in his gaze, then said, "You have nothing to worry about from me." She sat down in the driver's seat of her Mercedes Benz.

He closed the door. "I hope that I can trust you."

"I wouldn't do anything to hurt you, Colton. The truth is that I've fallen in love with you, but... all I can say is that it's your loss. We had a good time while it lasted."

Harini drove away, tears streaming down her face. She'd really believed in her heart that Colton was going to choose her. She could not believe he had chosen that *nobody*. Bailey didn't know what to do with a man like Colton. She didn't deserve him.

Chapter 10

"The boardwalk here is amazing," Bailey murmured. "I'm loving Atlantic City, especially the Steel Pier."

Colton laughed. "You were like a little kid on the rides."

"I haven't been on a ride in years until today. It reminded of my fair days back home."

"I was thinking that maybe we should get married," Colton said. "We can do it right here in Atlantic City."

Bailey eyed him. "Is that your way of proposing?"

"I love you and I don't want to spend another day apart from you."

"What's gotten into you?" she asked. "I know we've both been pretty busy, but we're good, baby."

Colton kissed her. "C'mon... why are we waiting? We've been together four years. Let's get married right now."

"What's the rush all of a sudden?" Bailey asked. "You're the one who wanted to have a wedding."

"The thought that I could lose you one day…"

"You're not going to lose me," Bailey interjected.

"I guess I'm just being selfish," Colton said before kissing her.

She embraced him. "I think it's really sweet, but you're going to have to come up with a more romantic proposal."

They laughed.

"C'mon, I want to buy some souvenirs," Bailey told him, leading Colton by the hand. "I saw some tee shirts that would be perfect for Maurie and Cass."

When they finished shopping, Bailey and Colton returned to their hotel room at Ballys.

"After dinner we going to the casino, right?" he asked.

"You know there's a concert tonight as well." Bailey sat on the edge of the bed and removed her shoes. "I don't know if we can still get tickets, but since we're here—we might as well try."

"I don't see why we can't do both," Colton responded. "We can stay up late and sleep in tomorrow."

Bailey held up a red and black strapless dress against her body. "What do you think? Should I wear this tonight?"

Colton broke into a grin. "Definitely."

Her cell phone rang.

"It's Harini," Bailey said.

"Don't answer it. We're on vacation."

"I can send her a quick text."

"Why?" Colton asked. "You're a grown woman. You don't need to report your whereabouts to Harini Samuels."

Bailey met his gaze. "You really don't like her, do you?"

"She's alright."

"Honey, I know you. You don't care for Harini and it's okay. She's the type of person you will either like or can't stand to be in the same room with her. But I can't deny that I've learned a lot from her. I bought all of the books she recommended, so I feel like I have a great start."

"Take what you've learned so far and just go for it. Submit your book to the publishers," Colton said. "What are you waiting for? You don't need her permission."

"I'm not looking for permission from Harini. I was only going to update her. She's my mentor."

Colton pulled her into his arms. "I don't want to talk about Harini anymore. This weekend is all about you and me. Let's make every moment count."

Smiling, Bailey murmured, "Agreed."

"THE DOCTOR WILL BE with you shortly."

"Thank you," Harini said. She sat down stoically to wait. It generally was at least ten to fifteen minutes before the doctor ever showed up. This time it was closer to a half-hour before the knock on the door came.

Her doctor entered, the chart in her hand. She looked at it briefly, then at her. "How long have you been pregnant?"

She shrugged her shoulders. "A month, maybe two. I took a home pregnancy test. I waited to come in because... because of what's happened in the past. I was afraid to get my hopes up."

"Lay back on the table and I'll take a look," she said.

Silently Harini climbed onto the small examination table and put her feet in the stirrups. The bright lights in the ceiling over her head shone into her eyes. She blinked.

"Take a deep breath."

She filled her lungs with air and held perfectly still against the searching intrusion of her doctor's fingers. Her touch was light and efficient and was gone in a moment.

Harini started to sit up, but Dr. Richard's hand against her shoulder stopped her. She lay quietly waiting.

"Why did you become pregnant, Harini?" she asked. "After the last one, I informed you that you could endanger your life."

Harini shrugged. "I want to have a baby. As a woman, I'd expect you to understand.

I've gotten everything I've ever wanted in life—except the chance to be a mother. I feel like my womb is cursed. I have no problem getting pregnant, but I can't carry to term. It's not fair."

Dr. Richards gave her a sympathetic smile, then said, "Get plenty of fresh air and rest. Refrain from sex for at least three months. Eat plenty of healthy foods." She scribbled a prescription and handed it to her. "Take this. I want to see you again in four weeks."

Harini looked at her. "Will I be able to carry this baby, Doctor? This time it feels different."

Dr. Richard kept her face impassive. "I am going to do what I can."

"Thank you," Harini said quietly.

A month had gone by since she last saw Colton. She had promised herself that he wasn't worth her time and energy, but her pregnancy gave Harini renewed hope.

"I GOT my first rejection letter today," Bailey announced.

"Baby, I'm sorry." Colton embraced her.

"I'm okay." She stepped out of his arms. "It was a nice one. The editor just didn't feel it was the right project for her."

"How many did you send out?"

"Four," Bailey responded. "I only need one person to say yes." She was still very hopeful about her writing. She wasn't going to let one rejection letter get her down.

"You're going to sell your book," Colton said to reassure her. "I can't explain it, but I know you're going to be this renowned author one day."

"The worst-case scenario is that I'll have to self-publish. I'm not going to give up on my dream."

"I'm glad to hear it." He swept her up into his arms. His

kiss held them bound by breath and soul. Carrying her through the apartment to her bedroom, he set her on her feet and in seconds they fell onto the bed covered in a soft comforter and a mountain of pillows.

Holding her close, he whispered, "I forgot the popcorn."

Bailey chuckled. "We didn't make any, silly."

"How are we going to watch a movie without popcorn?" Colton asked.

She sat up in bed. "Is this your way of saying you want me to make popcorn for you?"

"You don't have to do that," he told her. Reaching into his pocket, he pulled out a couple of candy bars. "We have these."

Bailey snuggled against Colton, entangling her legs with his. "I love moments like this," she murmured. "We don't have to do anything special—just laying here with you is enough."

They lay together, heartbeats thundered, and each breath was a sigh sifting into the quiet. The clock on the nightstand and the steady tick of seconds passing pounded out around them like a drumbeat.

Chapter 11

"Colton, thank you for coming."

"You made it sound more like an order," he responded.

"Harini, I meant what I said. What we had is over. Bailey and I are closer than ever. In fact, I plan on proposing to her."

"I hope you haven't gone out and bought a ring yet."

"Why?"

"There's something I need to tell you," Harini said, "that's why I asked you to come over. I went to the doctor earlier."

"Are you okay?" he asked.

"Wow. You actually sound concerned about me."

"I do care about you as a person. What's going on?"

"Colton, I'm pregnant."

"Excuse me?"

The pain in his expression wounded her to the core. He's just in shock, she told herself. It's going to be fine. Harini reached over to take his hand and press it to her stomach. "I'm going to have a baby... *your* baby."

"What am I supposed to do with this?" he asked, removing his hand.

Harini swallowed hard. "I can't go through this alone,

Colton. I've lost three babies. Like my other pregnancies, this one is high-risk."

"How do I know you're not lying to me?"

She handed him a piece of paper. "I figured you'd want proof. It's insulting that you think I'd lie about something like this. I'm not a desperate woman, Colton."

Looking at the information, he shook his head. "Bailey…"

"She has nothing to do with this," Harini stated. "You and I are the only two people that matter in this situation."

"So, you're expecting me to just dump Bailey?"

"What do you think is going to happen when she finds out that I'm carrying your child, Colton? There's no way she'd stay with you and you know it."

"Did you get pregnant deliberately? He asked.

Harini shook her head no. "If you think that, then you don't know me at all. This pregnancy came as a surprise to me. Just to be clear, I don't need *you*—I have more than enough money to raise this child on my own. My brother's here as well. If we have to do it alone—*we will*."

"I just need a couple of days to process this," Colton responded. "How far along are you?"

"About eight weeks."

"You've had a lot more time to get used to the idea. Why didn't you tell me when you suspected you were pregnant?"

"I wasn't sure, Colton. It was only confirmed this afternoon. To be honest, I was terrified to see my doctor. I was afraid she'd tell me that this pregnancy wasn't a viable one. I didn't want to lose another baby."

"So, what did she say?" Colton asked.

"I need to follow her instructions to the letter pretty much. She's going to be monitoring me closely. I need to avoid any and all stress." Harini looked at him and said, "I want this child more than anything else in this world."

"I can't believe this," Colton murmured.

"I'm sorry if this inconveniences you."

"Harini… I'm sorry if I'm not saying what you want to hear. This is just a lot for me to deal with right this moment. I need some time to process this."

"I understand."

"I thought you were on birth control."

"Nothing is a hundred percent, Colton. If you're thinking that this is some kind of trap—you're way off base. I don't need you in my life or to raise this child. It would've been easy for me to just go to a sperm bank."

"Look, I'm not trying to upset you, Harini. I just need time to deal with all this."

"Fine," she responded.

"I have to go," Colton said. "I'll call you in a couple of days."

Harini saw him to the door, locking it when he left.

"You're still up to your old tricks."

She turned around, arms folded across her chest. "Pip, I'm not in the mood."

"You lied to Colton," her brother accused. "You got pregnant on purpose despite the risks to your health."

"I want to be a mother." Harini took a sip of her water. "It's not like I'm getting any younger."

"You're twenty-seven years old."

"I want to have children before I'm thirty."

"Your health…"

"I don't care," she responded. "I'm having this child."

"Colton's not going to leave Bailey for you."

"He won't have to—she's gonna leave him. I know that much about Bailey."

"You think it's going to be that easy?"

"Yeah, I do," Harini said. "This baby will bring Colton and I closer together. You'll see. We're gonna be one big happy family. Of course, this means that you're gonna have to leave."

Pip shrugged in nonchalance. "This is about to get interesting."

"HOW'S THE JOB HUNT GOING?" Bailey asked Colton as he stepped aside to let her enter his apartment.

"I have couple of interviews lined up," He responded. "I hope I get the job with at least one of them. Some people have already been let go. I don't want to have to depend on a severance package."

"You'll find one," she assured him. "Just remember that you're not alone in this, Colton."

He walked over to a window and stared out.

Bailey followed him. "What's wrong?" she asked, studying his face. "You look troubled about something else. What's going on?"

"I just have a lot on my mind."

"Anything you want to talk about?"

Colton shook his head. "Not right now."

"If you're not up to seeing a movie tonight, we can do it another time."

"I don't deserve you," Colton said as he pulled her closer to him.

Bailey smiled. "You sure you're okay?"

"I will be."

"You know you can talk to me about anything."

"We're going to miss the first part of the movie if we don't leave now."

Bailey knew Colton well enough that he was really upset about something, but she didn't press him for more information. When he was ready to tell her—he would.

HARINI WAS GROWING IMPATIENT. It was time to take matters into her own hands. Having just received her publishing contract—she had to talk to Bailey. She took a deep breath, then picked up her cell phone.

"Hello."

"Bailey, it's Harini. How are you?"

"I'm fine. This is a nice surprise."

"The reason I'm calling is to see if I can come by your place this evening. There's something I need to discuss with you. Something deeply personal."

"Sure."

"I'm not interrupting any plans with Colton, am I?"

"No. He's actually out of town and won't be back until Thursday."

"Great," Harini said. She was more than a little irritated that she hadn't been told about Colton's little trip. He owed her that much. Three days passed since she'd told him about her pregnancy. She hadn't heard a word from him. "I'll see you around sevenish."

"See you then."

The call ended.

"Tonight, your life is going to change," Harini whispered.

"Have you heard from baby daddy?"

She turned to face her brother. "I wish you'd stop sneaking up on me. I hate it."

"You're in a mood."

"It's my hormones," Harini responded.

"Why did you do it?" Pip asked. "You know what the doctor told you the last time."

"I want a baby."

"I know that, sis. But your doctor warned you that you're more likely to experience preterm labor since you delivered premature babies in the last three pregnancies. She even told you the earlier a previous premature birth, it increases the chances that the next birth could come as early or even earlier."

"I'm not going to focus on the negative. I'm only sending positive vibes to this baby."

"I'm worried for you. I know how much you want to be a mother. I also know that there's something wrong that causes you to go into preterm labor. Placental abruption—that's what your doctor called it."

"Pip, I don't want to talk about this anymore," Harini said. "I'm pregnant and I want to focus on the joy of this wonderful miracle. I never thought I'd get another chance. I'm happy. So happy."

He smiled. "Then I'm thrilled for you, my dear sister."

"You're going to be an uncle. I already know you're going to be so protective of this child. I'm going to write as much as I can before this little angel comes. When he or she gets here—I want to focus on him or her." Harini broke into a grin. "Maybe I'll write some children's books. What do you think, Pip?"

"I think that's a great idea, sis."

Harini glimpsed a certain sadness in her brother's eyes. "It's gonna be okay. We're gonna be fine. I have such a good feeling; a peace about everything."

Chapter 12

Bailey cleaned up her apartment, hoping that Harini wouldn't notice the cheap particle board bookshelves, the used sofa she'd found at a flea market, and the worn carpeting. "Why should I care what she thinks? Harini didn't always have money," Bailey said to herself.

Her guest arrived fifteen minutes earlier than expected.

"Harini... hey."

"Thank you for seeing me." Harini's eyes traveled around the tiny apartment, but she didn't comment.

Bailey gestured toward the sofa. "We can sit over here and talk."

As soon as they were seated, Harini said, "I have some news I want to share with you. The first is that I just sold another book to Snyder and James. It's one they are really excited about it."

"That's wonderful," Bailey said, smiling. "I'm so happy for you. We're going to have to celebrate."

"I'm very excited."

"These are the moments I'm looking forward to, Harini.

I've done the final edits to my manuscript. I'm ready to start submitting it to publishers."

"That's another reason why I needed to talk to you."

"What is it?" Bailey wondered if Harini was about to suggest that she submit to her publisher. She could barely contain her excitement.

"I've done a lot of thinking about your story. The thing is that it's very similar to the book I have coming out."

Bailey stiffened. "What do you mean it's similar? You've never mentioned this before," she said.

"The point is that I'm telling you now." Harini stated without emotion. "I didn't want to discourage you after all the work you've done, but the more I think about it—you should come up with another story. Now, I'm not saying you can't put it out at some point…"

A knife twisted in Bailey's gut while she struggled to keep her mouth from gaping.

"How could you do this to me?" she demanded after finally finding her voice. "I t-thought you were my friend," Bailey said. "I can't believe I was that stupid."

Harini's eyes filled with an inexpressible sorrow. "Bailey," she whispered, "you've never been like the others. You've been almost—well, almost like a sister to me. It's important that you understand something. I didn't *steal* your story. No idea is unique, original, or owned by another person. It is not stealing to take an idea and rework it into your own." She spoke as if speaking to a child. "Don't let anyone tell you otherwise, and do NOT give up an idea because somebody tells you it's similar to another author."

"It would be different if you hadn't seen my synopsis, Harini. You intentionally did this to me. I trusted you and you betrayed me."

"You can submit your story to publishers, Bailey. Mine will come out first, however. It's already been assigned a pub date."

"Kaile was right about you." Bailey prided herself on being able to read people, but she'd missed one important fact—at the end of the day, people were only out for themselves.

Harini shrugged in nonchalance. "I'm a New York Times Bestseller. You... well, you're not even published. If it makes you feel better, I'll write you a check for two thousand dollars.

I'm sure you can come up with another idea for your book." She smiled. "I have faith in you."

"I don't want your money," Bailey snapped. "Do you really think offering me cash is going to make this right between us?" Tears prickled behind her eyes, and she squeezed her lids tight. She refused to let Harini see her cry.

"I really hope you aren't thinking of doing something stupid like making this public," Harini said. "But even if you do, no one will believe you anyway. You're a nobody."

Bailey sent her a sharp glare. "You're a horrible person."

"I understand why you'd think that." Harini took a sip of water. "Since we're being honest with one another, there's something else you need to know."

"What?"

"Colton and I... we've been sleeping together. We didn't mean for it to happen, but he and I... we were drawn to one another."

Hands clenched into fists, Bailey rose to her feet.

"I hope you don't intend on putting your hands on me," Harini said calmly. "Because I'll have you arrested for hitting a pregnant woman."

"You're evil and a liar," Bailey declared. "I don't believe a word you said about Colton. He would never hurt me like this."

"That's your first mistake... believing that any man won't hurt you. You think he really loves you? Colton cares for you, but love... I don't think so."

Unshed tears prickled painfully. The book of her heart;

someone she loved dearly, could be taken away from her and there wasn't a thing Bailey could do about it, but she was not about to let Harini in on her realization. "I promise that you'll answer for this one day."

"Bailey let's be mature about this." Harini's bland tone tried unsuccessfully to hide a touch of sarcasm. "If you're thinking of telling this little tale of yours—I'll make it known that you're angry with me because I took your man. People will see you as a woman scorned."

Fierce anger welled up in Bailey. "You're a miserable excuse for a human being. I don't know if you're lying about being pregnant—either way, it's the only reason I haven't punched you in the face."

"So much for maturity…"

Bailey picked up Harini's expensive designer purse and tossed it in the direction of the door. "Get out of here *now*."

Harini stood up. "I wish you much success with your writing."

Bailey uttered a string of profanity laced with threats of physical harm.

"Look…" Harini began.

"Without thinking, Bailey slapped Harini with the full force of her hand. "I don't want to hear another word you have to say."

Water glazed her eyes. "Owwww…" Harini gently touched her burning cheek.

"Say one word and I'll hit you again," Bailey warned. "Now get out of my apartment before I end up going to jail."

Harini brushed past her, walking briskly to the door.

Bailey slammed it close, then focused on calming herself.

In.

Out.

Just keep breathing in and out, she told herself over and over.

Don't think about anything but breathing.

Black dots danced in front of Bailey's eyes, her breathing so shallow she didn't think any oxygen was reaching her brain. She shifted her head a bit. "Breathe…" she whispered. "Breathe…"

She navigated over to the desk and tossed her manuscript into the trash.

Tears ran down her face. She couldn't fathom someone like Harini do this to her. Why would she do it? She was a renowned author. She was a fantastic writer. Why wasn't this enough for her?

Why am I letting her get way with this?

Sure, she could talk to an attorney, but there was really no use. The truth was that it wasn't possible under the law to copyright or protect an idea or title. What hurt Bailey was that Harini had stolen her idea, had most likely executed it better, and was able to sell it to her publisher. On top of that, Harini had also taken her man. That betrayal devastated Bailey to her core—that Colton had a large part in breaking her heart.

Bailey navigated to her bathroom and washed her face.

She wanted blood, but Bailey could not bring herself to hit a pregnant woman. Although Harini could've been lying—she didn't want to take the chance. Instead, she had allowed that snake to victimize her and worst, get away with it.

How could I be so stupid? I thought we were building a friendship… how Harini must have laughed at me. I must have looked so desperate to her.

Bailey admired Harini; considered her a literary role model, but the woman used her. She had also taught her a valuable lesson. Most people only pretended to be genuine, but they weren't. Colton's actions had only reinforced that truth.

"BAILEY HARGROVE DIDN'T DESERVE THIS," Pip stated. "None of it."

"You're *my* brother. I would think that you'd be happy for me. I have a new book that's going to redeem me; I have a baby on the way, and I have someone to share my life with… he's gorgeous, too."

"Colton doesn't love you."

"He's the father of my child," Harini responded. "He'll come to love me."

"Sis… you aren't going to keep getting away with stuff like this. You think you've won this battle with Bailey…" Pip shook his head. "I don't think so."

"That little mouse is just gonna run off and find somewhere to hide. She's not woman enough to take me on."

"I wouldn't put her out to pasture so quickly, sis."

Harini laughed. "I'm telling you that Bailey Hargrove is nothing I have to worry about. She had the opportunity to take me on last night, but she didn't. Not even when I told her about Colton and the baby."

"It was probably because you're pregnant," Pip said. "The minute she touched you—you would've had her arrested."

"You're right about that."

"So, you consider it bravery to hide behind your pregnancy?"

Harini glared at her brother. "You're trying to pick a fight with me."

"I'm simply stating the truth, sis."

"I don't have time to do this with you, so I'ma give you a pass." Harini walked briskly into her closet. "I need to change clothes. Colton's coming over."

"I certainly don't want to be around for this little celebration. If Mother and Father were here to see you right now…"

"Get out," Harini screamed. "They would be proud of me, too."

Silence.

She burst into tears. Pip had no right bringing their parents into this. He knew how it would make her feel.

Harini placed a hand to her belly. "It's okay, sweetie. I'm not going to let your mean ol' uncle upset me—not tonight."

"HEY BABE..." Colton greeted when he entered the apartment. "I called you earlier, but it went straight to voicemail." He eyed her. "What's wrong? Why are you crying?"

Bailey's gazed settled on him, studying his expression. "I had a conversation with Harini."

Surprised registered in his eyes, then disappeared as quickly as it had come. "What did she tell you?"

Bailey wiped away her tears. "What do you think she told me, Colton?"

"I'm sorry," he began. "I never meant for th—"

"What I don't understand is how you could do this to me."

"I messed up, Bailey. I ended things with her right before we left for Atlantic City."

"Is that why you were in such a hurry to get married?" she asked. "Because you were afraid I'd find out."

"I wanted to marry you because I love you."

Bailey disagreed. "More like you thought things would be better if we were married when I found out about you two."

"It was a mistake, baby."

"The only mistake was my trusting you." Bailey glared at him. "Did you know that she basically stole my storyline, too?"

"She did *what?*"

"You heard me. She took my book idea and there's nothing I can do about it. Her book will come out and so there's no chance of publishing mine. I can't believe I was such a fool." Bailey eyed him. "But you, Colton..." she shook her head.

"Harini told me that she's pregnant. How long have you known?"

"I just found out about the baby a couple of days ago, Bailey."

"When Harini told me that she'd been sleeping with you— I just knew it was a lie. I kept telling myself that you'd never do something like this to me. I really didn't believe her until I saw the expression on your face. Tell me… how long have you been seeing her?"

"It only lasted about a month, then I ended things with Harini. Bailey, I love you. I—"

"*No*," she interjected. "No, you don't. There's no way you can love me. Because if you did, you wouldn't have cheated on me."

"I have no excuse for doing what I did, but I don't love Harini. I want to be with you."

Bailey shook her head. "There's no coming back from this, Colton."

"Babe, I had no idea about the book—this isn't the type of woman I'd want in my life."

"Well if she's telling the truth about the baby, she's going to be a part of your life forever."

"I'll be a father to my child, but that's it. You are the woman I want to marry."

"Hear me when I say this. I don't want to marry you," Bailey said. "You've destroyed my trust and without that, a relationship can't work."

"I'm sorry."

"Colton, please don't insult me with an apology," she interjected. "Just get out. Get out of my apartment." Summoning as much strength as she could, Bailey pointed to the door. "I need you to leave. Get out *now*."

"Please…"

"Go." His words meant nothing to her now.

Shoulders hung low, Colton had no choice but to leave. When he exited, Bailey knew this was the last time she'd see him.

This was it. Everything that had gone before was like nothing. Now Bailey had to live with her poor choices where Harini was concerned. Kaile had tried to warn her, but she wouldn't listen. Instead, Bailey chose to believe that her forewarning had been born out of jealousy.

Her breath was coming in gasps now. Black spots sped across Bailey's vision, racing one another from side to side. Before she could give in to the scream building in her throat, Bailey closed her eyes. She took a deep breath and tried to clear the pain from her chest.

Chapter 13

"How could you hurt Bailey like that?" Colton demanded when walked into her home. "What we did was bad enough. How could you steal her story?"

"First of all, you need to get your story straight," Harini sniped. "I didn't do anything wrong. Second, you're the wrong person to sit in judgment of me. You cheated on her."

"We were both wrong. Bailey didn't deserve what we've done to her." Colton sent her a sharp glare. "She worked really hard on that book."

"And Bailey can still put it out," Harini responded. "Mine will come out first though." She slipped her hand in his. "I was thinking that we could get married before the baby's born and—"

"Whoa… Harini, I don't want to marry you," Colton said, snatching his hand away.

Puzzled, she said, "We're going to have a baby. I just figured you'd want to raise this child together."

"After what you've done… there's no way I'd marry you," Colton responded. "I will support you through this pregnancy, but that's it. After the baby's born, we'll work out some type of custody arrangement."

"What exactly are you saying?"

"I thought I was pretty clear, Harini. Outside of this child, I want nothing to do with you."

"I understand that you're angry right now," Harini said, "We can revisit this topic after you've calmed down some."

"I need you to understand what I'm saying," Colton stated. "There will never be anything between us. Not after what you've done to Bailey. It was a mistake getting involved with you in the first place."

Shaking her head in denial, Harini whispered, "You don't mean that."

"Oh, but I do."

She placed a hand to her stomach. "So, you would selfishly deny your child the family he or she deserves. This baby shouldn't be punished for what you and I did."

"I will be a part of my child's life. I don't have to be married to you—we can co-parent."

"I won't accept that," Harini stated. "My child deserves to be raised in a two-parent home. You will either be in this baby's life on a full-time basis or not at all."

"Getting involved with you was foolish on my part. I've lost Bailey because of it, but I won't lose my child."

"Then I suggest you think long and hard about this decision."

Colton headed toward the door.

"I mean it," Harini said, following him. "I will take my child and disappear. We will raise this baby as a family or I'll do it as a single mother."

He left without a response.

"Didn't go quite the way you planned, huh?" Pip questioned from behind her.

Harini turned around to face her brother. "He's upset right

now. Colton will come around, especially if he wants to be a part of his child's life."

"He loves Bailey."

"She won't take him back," Harini responded.

"Doesn't mean Colton will come running to you."

"And it doesn't mean that he won't, Pip." Harini sat down on the leather sofa. "Just watch. Colton's gonna come around to my way of thinking. I have so much more to offer him. Pip, you should've seen that dump she called a home. It was disgusting."

"Somehow I don't think that mattered to him. I'm also sure her apartment isn't as bad as you're making it out to be. You do tend to exaggerate. But regardless, Colton and Bailey will work through this or he will move on. Either way this man doesn't end up with you."

"You underestimate me, Pip. Just like our parents did."

"Listen to me—you can't win when you play the game of deception. Oh, it might look like you're winning, sis, but the truth is that while you may get a taste of victory; in the end you are not victorious."

"Why should I listen to you?" Harini asked.

"Because I'm the voice of reason. I'm your conscious."

"Whatever... I'm done with this conversation."

HARINI WASN'T surprised when Colton showed up the next morning. She pretended that the exchange they'd had the day before never took place. "I was just about to have breakfast. Care to join me?"

He followed her into the kitchen.

It was obvious by his red eyes that Colton hadn't slept all night. Silently he sat down at the table.

Harini reappeared with two plates laden with toast, scrambled eggs, and bacon.

"You cooked?" Colton asked, his surprise evident.

"I did," Harini said with a grin. "I shocked myself." She poured some tea into his cup.

"Where's Pip?"

"He's not here," Harini responded.

"He's traveling again?"

She nodded. "My brother loves to travel." Harini paused a moment, then said, "I'm sure you didn't come over here to discuss Pip. Why did you come?"

"I thought about the threat you made last night," Colton said, "I'm not about to let you even think you can force me into something I don't want. I'm not in love with you, Harini. I don't particularly *like* you right now. There's no way you're going to force my hand when it comes to marriage."

Harini took a long sip of her tea. "Apparently, you misunderstood me. I made no threats, Colton."

"So that there are no more misunderstandings, Harini... let me be clear. I will be in my child's life, even if it means taking you to court."

"I don't want to fight with you. I would like for my pregnancy to be a stress free as possible."

"I'm not trying to upset you."

"You haven't," Harini said. "Believe it or not, I understand the position you're in, Colton. I am well aware of how difficult this must be for you. I do believe that you'll come to do what's right."

Colton thought he'd won this round, but Harini knew better. She decided to hold her tongue for now, but she would get her way in this. She would marry him before their child was born. Harini refused to accept that he would choose Bailey over her. She had so much more to offer him.

"When is your next doctor visit?" Colton inquired.

"Next month," Harini responded. She stuck a forkful of scrambled eggs into her mouth.

"Text me the date and time so I can put it on my calendar. I want to be there."

"Is this out of concern for our child or do you want proof that I'm really pregnant?"

"Both," Colton stated. "That piece of paper you showed me could have been faked."

Harini glared at him. "I'm not desperate to have you in my life. I don't need you, Colton. I've sold a lot of books; have a couple of movie adaptations, and I've made a lot of money. You're the father of this child I'm carrying. You either want to be in our lives or you don't. I just need to know which."

"I will be here for my child, Harini."

Colton's tone brooked no argument. She decided it was best to just let the subject drop for now. She didn't want to force his hand—it was too soon. If she played her hand smart, she would end up with the man.

———

THE LAST SEVEN days had been surreal. Like something out of a horrible nightmare that not even Bailey's own subconscious would torture her with.

The fragrant steam rising from a plate of crispy fried chicken in the center of the table stirred up a rumble in Bailey's empty stomach.

"I knew there wasn't something right about Harini Samuels," Cassidy said. "But I never would've imagined that she would be this conniving. What I'm shocked about is Colton. I never thought he'd be unfaithful to you."

They sat opposite one another at the dining room table, a southern feast of fried chicken, savory smell of macaroni and cheese, turnip greens, and cornbread spread out between them. Although she didn't have much of an appetite, the mouthwatering aromas sent Bailey's nose into ecstatic twitches.

The air conditioner in the apartment worked overtime to try to dispel the summer humidity. The green and white curtains at the kitchen window above the sink had been pulled closed, but the sun still radiated heat through them. Bailey dabbed at her damp forehead with a napkin before spooning macaroni and cheese onto her plate.

"This is the first real meal I've eaten since this nightmare began."

"I figured as much," Cassidy said. "That's why I cooked all this food."

"Thank you for getting me out of my apartment."

"I know Colton broke your heart and Harini betrayed you, but the pain will eventually go away."

"I know what you're saying is right, Cass. It's just that it hurts so bad right now. It even hurts to breathe."

"You shouldn't let what Harini's actions stop you from putting out the book you wrote."

Bailey shook her head no. "I trashed it."

"Why?"

"It's tainted to me now."

"Bailey, that was a wonderful story."

"I don't want anything to do with writing—not anymore." She bit into the drumstick.

"People are only out for themselves."

Cassidy wiped her mouth with a paper napkin. "Don't let what happened stop you from fulfilling your dream. You can't give Harini that kind of power over you. That skank ain't worth it. Success is your best revenge."

Bailey took a sip of her soda. "She won. People like them always do."

"Not everybody is like her, Bailey. There are still some good people in the world."

"I don't want to talk about this anymore," Bailey stated. "I have to do what's best for me. That's why I'm moving back to North Carolina."

Cassidy was surprised. "Are you seriously leaving?"

"Yes. There's a position available in the Raleigh office." Bailey couldn't wait to leave Philadelphia. She wanted to be as far from Colton and Harini as possible."

"Are you still interested in moving to the commercial side?"

Bailey nodded. "As soon as there're an opening, I'm going to apply. I've even been thinking about going back to school—getting a graduate degree."

"Really?"

"Yes," she responded. "I need to stay busy."

"When do you leave?"

"I'm scheduled to start work in two weeks, so I'll be out of my apartment this Saturday.

I need to find a place to live and get settled in Raleigh as soon as possible."

"I'm going to really miss you, Bailey. Why don't we go out on Friday? We need a girls' night out."

Bailey wiped her mouth with her napkin. "I don't know... I'll think about it."

Cassidy pressed her lips tight and raised her chin high. "I can't stop you from leaving Philly, but we're having that girls' night."

Bailey knew without a doubt that her friend meant it. "Thank you for dinner and all that you're trying to do, Cass. I really appreciate it." She knew she could trust Cassidy and Maurie—they were the only two people Bailey would ever trust. She would never allow anyone else to get close to her again.

"You're welcome."

"Going out with the girls might do me good. I'm looking forward to it."

Cassidy smiled. "We're going to have a good time. I promise." She sat back in her chair and sucked in a loud breath, rubbing the round bump of her belly. "This little one doesn't like the heat either. He's kicking me."

"Where? Let me feel."

Cassidy took Bailey's hand and placed it on her side.

She sat breathless for a moment. Finally, Bailey felt a firm poke beneath her fingers.

"Oh, my goodness! I can't believe you're going to be a mommy in five months."

"I know… I'm still getting used to the idea myself. Joe is over the moon about being a father."

"Harini's pregnant," Bailey announced. "At least that's what she's claiming."

"Is she saying that Colton's the father?" Cassidy asked.

"Of course."

"I hope he has enough sense to have a paternity test done." Cassidy arched and placed a fist in the small of her back for support. "This is unforgivable."

"I have to forgive him, Cass. It's not for him—it's for me."

"Now you sound like a preacher's kid."

"Forgiveness isn't for the offender. It's for the person who was hurt. If I truly want to move on, then I have to forgive Colton and Harini, but right now… I just can't do it."

"If I were in your shoes, I'd never be able to forgive him," Cassidy stated.

"I'm just taking it one day at a time." Bailey took a drink of water. "I don't even want to think about them." Her eyes teared up. "I loved Colton. That's what's so hard about this."

"I hope I don't run into Harini anytime soon," Cassidy said. "I will knock that witch all the way out."

Bailey wiped her mouth on her napkin. "If she wasn't pregnant…" She pushed away from the table. "I've never hated anyone, but Harini… I really *hate* that woman."

"Don't waste any emotion on her. She's totally not worth it."

After a moment, Bailey responded, "You're right, Cass. Harini's not worth it. But I have to say this—I'm going to make her pay for what she did to me. I mean it with every fiber of my being and it will be when she least expects it."

Chapter 14

One month after moving back to Raleigh, Bailey received a call from her mother.

"Your aunt passed away this morning."

"Mama, I'm so sorry." Her eyes filled with tears. "How are you handling all this?"

"I'm going to miss June, but I take comfort that she's no longer in pain and living with confusion. I'm bringing her home. She wanted to be buried next to our parents."

"When will you get here?"

"We're flying out in the morning. I've already contacted the funeral home. They will meet the plane."

"I'll be there, too."

"I called your sisters. They're coming home for the funeral."

Although her aunt's death was not a joyous event, she was excited for the reunion of family.

"I hope you don't mind if I stay with you until I find a place of my own."

"Of course not... Mama, you can stay as long as you like." Bailey looked forward to seeing her mother.

"You okay, Bailey?"

She glanced over at her co-worker. "My aunt passed away."

"I'm so sorry for your loss."

"Thank you. My mama's bringing her body home tomorrow. The funeral will be here in Raleigh."

"Why don't you take the rest of the day off? It's not really busy."

Bailey forced a smile. "It's always busy in the claims department, but I am going to leave. I can't really think of anything other than my Aunt June."

"Go home. I'll cover your desk."

"Thanks so much." Bailey gathered her purse and keys.

She exited the building after a quick conversation with her supervisor.

The last time she'd visited her aunt, Colton had gone with her. He comforted her as she cried afterward. Bailey hated seeing her mother's sister in such an incapacitated state.

Colton had reached out to her twice in the past month. She sent the calls straight to voicemail. There was nothing to be said at this point, she decided. Bailey could never trust him again.

"I WAS THINKING we could go shopping," Harini suggested when she and Colton left the doctor's office.

"Don't you think it's too soon to buy baby stuff?" he asked.

She hid her disappointment that Colton didn't seem as excited as she was about the baby. The pregnancy was confirmed, so he knew she hadn't lied to him. "I thought we could get a few things or at least get an idea of how we'd like to decorate the nursery."

"I'm not in the mood to shop," Colton said. "And I'll leave

the decorating to you. You can even decorate the second bedroom at my place, too."

"What are you talking about?" Harini inquired. "Why do we need to decorate a room at your apartment?"

"The baby will be with me sometimes. He or she will have a room there."

Harini bit her bottom lip in frustration. "Colton, there's more than enough room in my condo. It would make more sense for you to just move in there. We can have separate bedrooms if you want."

"What about Pip?"

"He's been talking about moving out. He fancies living somewhere in Europe. Colton, why are you being so difficult? You thought I was lying about the pregnancy. Now you know that I wasn't." Harini's voice softened. "I know that you care for me."

"When you took advantage of Bailey like that... that changed whatever I may have felt for you."

"I didn't do anything to that whiney little girl," Harini snapped. "So, what... I took her story idea and made it mine. Do you think she came up with it all by herself? *She didn't.* There are only so many plots in the world. My book is nothing like the one she wrote—the only difference is that mine is much better and it's going to be published. I'm not saying she wouldn't be able to get a publisher. It just won't do as well as mine will."

"You really are a piece of work, Harini." Colton slipped on his shades. "If you weren't carrying this child, I'd never have anything else to do with you."

"Oh, now you want to play the loyal boyfriend," she stated. "It's too late now. You're never gonna get Bailey back."

"And you will never get me back into your bed. I'll see you at the next doctor's appointment."

"Excuse me?"

"I don't want anything to do with you. I am only here for my child."

Harini's eyes welled with tears. "You don't mean that."

"Yeah… I do," Colton responded. "I'll take the subway home."

"I can drop you off."

"The truth is that I don't want to be around you right now."

"Colton let's go back to my place and talk. We can work this out."

"No."

"I have to avoid all stress," Harini murmured. She placed a hand to her belly. "I don't want to fight with you."

"Then just let me go. I'll give you a call later."

"Colton, I really don't want all this tension between us. I understand that you're upset with me, but can we put all that aside until after the baby's born?"

"I'll call you later."

Harini sighed. Colton was stubborn and not as easy to manipulate as she'd originally thought. *I'm going to have to give him more time to get over Bailey. By the time I give birth, he and I should be much closer. Colton and I have to work this out. We have to raise our child together. Children deserve two loving parents. His gorgeous looks, my beauty and brains—our baby is very lucky.*

During the drive home, she thought about Bailey. She'd managed to turn Colton against her, and that angered Harini.

"Stay calm," she whispered. "You can't upset the baby."

Harini forced her thoughts to something more pleasant—a theme for the baby's room.

———

"THE SERVICE WAS NICE," Bailey told her mother. "Aunt June

would have loved it. She always used to say that she wanted her homegoing to be a celebration of her life."

"I didn't expect so many of her friends to travel from Kansas. My sister made friends everywhere she went. That was the kind of person she was."

Bailey agreed.

"Have you heard from Colton? I kinda expected him to show up for the funeral."

"He's reached out a couple of times, Mama but I haven't talked to him. If I'd told Colton about Aunt June's passing—he probably would've come."

"What he did to you—it's a hard pill to swallow, but I know he loved you, Bailey."

"How could he?" she questioned. "He cheated with the same woman who took my idea—the woman I thought was my mentor. I thought she was my friend."

"One thing for sure… you and she have different ideas about friendship."

"You're right about that, Mama. Harini doesn't know what it means to be a friend. She simply uses people for whatever she wants, then discards their feelings like yesterday's trash. If you'd seen her that night… she was actually gloating."

"Better you find out now rather than later."

"I feel so stupid," Bailey said, "People tried to warn me about her, but I wouldn't listen. I'll never make that mistake again."

"Ain't no point in living in the past. You know the type woman she is now. As for

Colton—he wasn't thinking with his brain. I'm sure she manipulated him just like she did you."

"They're having a baby, Mama."

"Girl, that was a trap plain and simple."

"Well, it's Colton's problem. Not mine," Bailey said with a

slight shrug. "If he hadn't been messing around with her—there would be no baby."

"He's human. He made a mistake."

"Mama, I can't trust Colton. Not after this."

"He loves you, Bailey."

"He'll get over it," she responded. "What we had ended when Colton got involved with Harini."

"Do you still love him?"

Bailey thought about her mother's question. "I don't think so. This betrayal destroyed my feelings for Colton." She closed her eyes as tears burned and the familiar taste of bitterness surged up the back of her throat. Deep down, Bailey hoped Colton and Harini would be miserable together for a lifetime.

Rebuilding trust and intimacy that has been stolen was not going to be easy, but Bailey knew it was doable. The truth was that she wasn't ready to forgive either of them. Bailey was still too angry, and she didn't know if she would ever stop feeling this way. It was her anger that fueled her—gave her the strength to crawl out of bed each morning.

———

MAURIE CAME DOWN to Raleigh to celebrate Bailey's birthday in November. They went to the Big Easy in Cary for dinner.

"Remember I told you that I have a cousin living here," Maurie said. "I hope you don't mind, but I invited my cousin. I haven't seen Trace in a while."

Bailey gave a slight shrug. "No, that's fine."

"So, how are you doing? *Really?*"

"I'm okay," she responded. "Some days are better than others."

"Have you heard from Colton lately?" Maurie asked in a

tone that gave Bailey the impression she was testing the waters by bringing up her ex.

"No, but I don't expect to hear from him anymore," Bailey responded, settling back in her seat. "I haven't responded to any of his calls since I left. He and Harini are having a child together. Colton needs to focus on them, because there's no chance of us ever getting back together."

"I always thought you two would get married. I know he doesn't love Harini."

"I thought we'd end up married one day, too," Bailey confessed. "I never thought of Colton seeing someone else. I realize now that I was very naïve. I've been thinking about my dad lately and the conversations we used to have about purity. Maybe if I'd made him wait—we would've been married by now."

"Here comes Trace now," Maurie said, putting an end to their conversation.

Her friend never mentioned that her cousin had gorgeous black hair with just enough curl to make a woman's fingers itch with the need to ruffle through it. Maurie never said that he had sexy eyes with long dark lashes that a woman might covet. Or that Trace had broad shoulders, a well-built frame and long legs that would easily turn a woman's head in his direction.

Maurie made the introductions. "This is Trace Thornton. Trace, this is my friend Bailey Hargrove."

She smiled. "It's very nice to meet you, Trace." Bailey could hardly take her eyes off him.

He smiled back at her and she felt the warmth of it deep in the pit of her stomach.

"Trace's mom and my mother are sisters."

"That must be Miss Peggy then," Bailey said with a grin. "I met her when she came for Mrs. Raymond's surprise birthday party. I picked her up from the airport."

"Small world," he murmured. "I hate I missed that party. I was in California for a wedding. Best man duties."

"You missed a really nice party."

"I heard," Trace responded. His gaze remained on Bailey.

She pretended not to notice. It was too soon for her to think about dating. Bailey was afraid that she would never trust another man. Her heart was too fragile after the heartache inflicted by Colton.

"You're coming for Thanksgiving, right?" Maurie asked her cousin. "Your mother and brothers will all be in Philly. We're going to the parade that morning."

"I'll be there," Trace responded.

"I've always wanted to see it in person," Bailey said. "I was looking forward to going this year, but I'm back in North Carolina." She gave a small laugh. "At least I'll be nice and warm and not wading through a crowd."

"Why don't you come up for the holiday?" Maurie suggested. "You and your mother. We'd love to have you."

"Thanks for the invitation, but Mama just wants to have a small dinner at home. She really misses Aunt June and my sisters. I think she's missing my dad most of all. Thanksgiving were a big deal when he was alive."

While they ate, Trace actively engaged her in conversation. Bailey was surprised they shared so many common interests.

"Bailey, I'm hoping I'll get the opportunity to see you again," Trace said after paying the check.

She smiled. "I work long hours but here's my number." Bailey handed him a business card.

"Well now...," Maurie said.

"Are you playing matchmaker?" Bailey asked. "Did you invite Trace to see if we'd hit it off?"

"No, I simply wanted to see my cousin while I was in town. I wasn't trying to hook you two up."

"I believe you."

"It wasn't my intent, but I like the way you two were interacting." Maurie paused a moment before asking, "So, is there a tiny grain of interest in my cousin? Did I tell you that he's a psychiatrist? He has a good job, girl."

Laughing, Bailey responded, "He's gorgeous, but I have to be honest. I'm not sure it was a good idea giving him my number. I'm just not in the frame of mind to start dating again."

"Give him a chance, Bailey. Just get to know Trace. It's not like you're making a lifelong commitment. I know he's my cousin, but he's a really good man."

"I thought the same thing about Colton."

"Trace is honorable. He's always been that way."

"I'm not promising anything, Maurie, but the most that can come out of this is friendship."

"You're going to find love again."

"Maurie, I'm fine. Love is how people manipulate you. I've had enough of that to last me a lifetime." Bailey stole a peek at her. "Don't give me that look. I'm good."

They left the restaurant and drove back to Bailey's apartment.

Her mother was in the living room reading the Bible when they walked inside.

"I bought you dinner," she announced.

"You didn't have to do that, but I appreciate it."

"Mama, you're too thin. I'm worried about you."

"I'm fine, sugar."

"You'd tell me if you're not feeling well."

"I would," her mother responded. "I think I'm still just dealing with June's death. You know we were real close."

"I know, Mama. It's just that you don't seem like yourself."

"I'll be fine, baby girl."

"I can tell that you think something's going on with your

mom," Maurie said when they were upstairs in Bailey's bedroom.

"She doesn't have much of an appetite and she's not sleeping at night. At first, I thought that it was just grief from losing her sister. Now, I'm not sure…"

"Your mom might be going through a little depression," Maurie stated. "My mother went through it when she lost her father and my dad."

"I hope it's nothing serious," Bailey said. "My emotions are still all over the place. I don't think I can handle anything else."

"Don't let this bitterness eat you up. I know you're hurting and it's hard to forgive, but fight through it, Bailey."

"I'm filled with fury. I'm still very angry with Colton and Harini."

"I know," Maurie said. "Anybody would feel the same way, but you're staying there in all that pain. You need to move on."

"Since everything happened, I've thought about all that my father used to tell me—what he preached on. I've even tried to give it to God, but all I want to do is find a way to hurt Harini."

"You want revenge."

"I do."

"You know what the Bible says, Bailey. You have to trust that someday it will come full circle—Harini will get exactly what she deserves. Colton's probably already getting his—he has that witch for a baby mama."

They burst into laughter.

Chapter 15

There was a sharp twinge of pain in her back, and Harini swayed dizzily. She reached quickly for her desk and held on to it until the dizziness passed.

The dizzy spell passed, and she went back to working on the new book. Harini wanted to have it completed a couple of months before her June due date, even though the deadline wasn't due until August. She wanted to focus entirely on her child when he or she was born.

When the dizziness didn't completely dissipate, Harini decided to lie down for a while and try to rest.

The condo was very still, and in the dark of her room, Harini found herself listening for every sound. She wondered if Pip had vanished to someplace secret. He never told her where he went in those times he left her alone.

She wanted to call Colton, but Harini knew he would think she was trying to manipulate him.

After a few minutes, the pain in her back subsided and she began feeling better. Harini forced herself to remain calm. She refused to let fear take control.

Harini considered calling her doctor but decided to wait.

I've been under a lot of stress. I'll just stay in bed for the rest of the day. Tomorrow even. I'll do whatever I have to do to save this baby.

"Positive vibes…" she murmured. "Everything is gonna be alright."

Harini drifted off to sleep.

Intense cramping woke her out of her nap, forcing a wave of panic to wash over her. "Nooo…"

She grabbed her phone and called Colton.

"Something's wrong," Harini said when he answered. "I need you."

"Where are you?"

"I'm at home."

"I'll be right there," Colton said. "Are you in bed?"

"Y-yes."

"Stay there. Do you have a spare key somewhere?"

"No… I can get up long enough to let you in. Please hurry."

Harini was grateful that he hadn't questioned her or treated her as if she were lying. His concern seemed genuine.

Colton arrived ten minutes later. His office wasn't that far from where she lived.

"You look pale," he told her before picking her up and laying her on the sofa. "Have you called your doctor?"

Nodding, Harini said, "I'm waiting on her to call me back."

"I don't think we should wait. I'm taking you to the hospital right now."

She felt something wet crawling down her leg. Water sprang in her eyes. "Colton…"

He eyed her. "What's wrong?"

"I'm bleeding." Tears streamed down her face. "My baby…"

Colton sprang into action. He called for an ambulance, then proceed to try to comfort Harini. "The paramedics will be here soon. You're going to be okay. I need you to just lay here and relax."

He stroked her face gently. "Stay calm. It's going to be fine."

Paramedics arrived and immediately went to work assessing the situation.

The placed her on a gurney and transported through the building to the ambulance.

Harini barely noticed the bleeps from a monitor, the paramedic in the back with her speaking to a doctor over the radio. Her focus was on the wellbeing of her unborn child. She was grateful to have Colton by her side. His presence had a calming effect, although she was still fearful. Not for herself, but for the child she carried.

As soon as she arrived at the hospital, lights pricked at Harini's eyes as she was taken through a hiss of automatic doors to a room in the emergency area.

Colton held her hand while she underwent a round of questions pertaining to her health, fetal monitoring, and an ultrasound, while they waited for the doctor to arrive.

They didn't have too long to wait.

"Hello I'm Dr. Watson."

After asking a few questions and a quick examination, he said, "You have a subchorionic hematoma."

"What's that?" Colton inquired.

"It's a fancy way of saying that I have blood clots between the placenta and my uterus," Harini explained. "I went through this the last time."

Dr. Watson went on to explain that she had blood clots in several locations. "This is a high-risk situation," he was saying. "A lot will depend on whether we can control the hemorrhaging."

"The baby…" Harini struggled to sit up.

"Please, Miss Samuels, you must try to lie very still." Dr. Watson protectively pressed his arm over her chest.

"Save my baby," she pleaded.

"We're going to do everything we can to make sure that you and the baby are okay," he said, patting her arm.

A wiry, fortyish nurse with blond hair and a heart-shaped face plumped Harini's pillow, keeping up reassuring chitchat as she checked vital signs. "Everything's going to be okay, honey. I'm going to strap on this device to monitor the baby." She went about the procedure in a confident manner.

"Please save my baby," Harini whispered, tears streaming down her face.

Colton planted a kiss on her cheek. "Just try to relax. You need to stay calm."

She looked up at him. "I'm scared." Harini closed her eyes and began praying in earnest. "Please God, don't take my child. Let me keep this one. Please…"

―――――――

BAILEY RAN nervous fingers down the front of the purple blouse she'd paired with some black pants. She'd actually put on not only mascara but also a touch of lipstick for the first time in months. It was a special occasion.

She had a date.

Trace called her two days after they met and from that moment forward, they talked on a daily basis. Mostly about superficial topics because Bailey refused to let down her guard. Eventually, Trace found a way around the wall she'd erected.

She had just finished applying her makeup when the doorbell sounded. Grinning, she opened the door.

Trace smiled at her. "You look beautiful."

"Thank you," Bailey responded. "You clean up nice yourself, Dr. Thornton."

He presented her with a bouquet of flowers. "These are for you."

"Maurie must have told you that orchids are my favorites."

"She did," he confessed. "I wanted to impress you."

"I'm impressed that you went to all this trouble."

Within minutes of entering the restaurant, Trace and Bailey were led to a table for two near a huge window.

"How do you like living in Cary?" she asked.

"I love it," Trace responded. "I've always liked North Carolina. We used to come down to Wilmington every summer."

"What brought you back to Raleigh?"

"Things didn't work out the way I thought they would, so I came home. This is where I belong." Bailey glanced down at the menu, then back at him. "Maurie told me that you used to teach high school."

"I did. I taught after I graduated college. Two years later, I was ready for a new chapter in my life, so I enrolled in medical school to study psychiatry. I've always had an interest in human behavior."

Bailey looked around the restaurant. "Being out with you is forcing me into a new chapter in my life. You're the first person I've been out with since my last relationship ended."

He laughed. "I hope it's one you are enjoying."

Smiling, she murmured, "So far so good."

"Here we are." The waitress with a name tag that read Marie set their plates in front of them.

Bailey's stomach rumbled as she gazed down at the stuffed baked chicken with roasted vegetable, mashed potatoes and gravy. "This looks yummy."

"It is," Trace said. "My sister-in-law is a wonderful cook. This is her restaurant."

"Really? How long has this place been in business?"

He nodded. "Almost a year."

A stunning woman wearing a white uniform approached the table. "Hello."

"Bailey, this is Michele. She's the owner and my brother's better half."

Smiling, she responded. "It's so nice to meet you, Michele. This chicken is delicious."

"I'm glad you're enjoying it."

When they were alone again, Trace said, "Now, tell me everything there is to know about Bailey Hargrove."

She grinned. "I'm not sure the meal will be long enough." Bailey tried to focus on the conversation, but it was hard to focus on his words when she wanted to fall into the warmth of his eyes.

"Maurie told me that you're a writer."

"Not anymore." Bailey sliced off a piece of chicken and stuck it in her mouth.

"Why not?"

Meeting his gaze, she said, "It's not something I really want to talk about, Trace."

He didn't press her. "Okay. We have much more we can discuss. I'm not one to beat around the bush. I like you and I'd really want to get to know you better."

"I'd like that, too." Bailey relaxed and settled back in her chair. "So, what else did Maurie tell you about me?"

"Just that you were one of her closest friends and that I'd better not do anything to hurt you. She was adamant about that."

Bailey felt bad over the way she'd responded earlier. "Trace, I apologize for being so abrupt when you mentioned my being a writer. I had a bad experience when I was in Philly. A woman I thought of as a mentor… she actually turned out to be a snake. She stole my storyline and made it her own. There's nothing I can do about it because you can't copyright an idea."

"I'm sorry you had to experience something like that. I know firsthand what it feels like to have someone betray you."

"I accept my responsibility in this situation. I really pursued the relationship because I thought we could build a friendship while she mentored me. My friend Cass tried to warn me about her, but I refused to listen."

"Is that why you stopped writing?"

"Partly but the other reason is that I just haven't been inspired." Bailey cleared her throat, then said, "I want to know more about you, Trace. Do you enjoy sports?" She didn't want to spend her evening talking about herself.

"I do. I'm a huge fan of football and basketball."

"So am I," Bailey responded. "Are you a Panthers fan?"

"I am."

"That's great. I plan to see as many of the home games I can."

"Will you marry me?"

Bailey laughed. "Only if you can cook."

"Actually, I can."

"What's your specialty?"

"I was born and raised in New Orleans," Trace said, "I would have to say my gumbo, shrimp and grits, and jambalaya are my specialties, but I can cook just about anything. My mama made sure all of us learned to cook."

"How many siblings do you have?"

"I have three brothers. What about you?"

"I have two sisters. No brothers."

"So, you have a brother living here?"

"Not yet," Trace responded. "My brother is still in Germany. He's in the Air Force. Retiring this month. Michele came stateside last August to get the kids in school and the restaurant up and running."

Bailey was enjoying Trace's company. She hadn't laughed so much in a long time, it seemed.

At the end of their evening, Trace was a perfect gentleman. He walked her to the door, planted a chaste kiss on her cheek, then asked if he could see her the following evening.

It was a perfect first date.

EMOTIONALLY DRAINED, too numb for more tears, Harini sagged against the cushions of the arm chair, the lone piece of furniture except for the crib positioned diagonally across the room. The lingering dusk of the January evening threw darkening shadows, but she made no move to turn on the lamp.

Cradling her head in her hands, Harini sat slumped, still wearing the black crepe dress that she'd worn to the funeral.

Harini was alone in the nursery—she didn't want anyone to intrude into the silence as she faced her reality—the death of her child; a death she'd never be able to reconcile as long as she lived.

Tears and a thick lump in her throat prevented her from screaming. She could hear people speaking downstairs, a spark of laugher here and there.

There's nothing to laugh about, Harini thought. There was no reason to be happy about anything. Especially when her life was steeped in misery.

The nauseating scent of the flowers, groups of them, arranged around the tiny white coffin still permeated Harini's nostrils, making every breath a nauseating pulsation. She could still feel her son's premature body from when she held him in her arms. She recalled praying over and over for his little chest to rise up and down, but to no avail. Eyes closed, he had looked as if he were in a peaceful sleep.

Why did this keep happening? she asked herself over and over. Four pregnancies; three miscarriages and one stillbirth. In order to stop the hemorrhaging, a hysterectomy had to be performed. There would be no more babies.

Selfish deceptions? With a heavy heart, she released a long sigh. *Why do my children have to pay the price for my mistakes?*

"I thought I'd find you up here?"

Harini looked up find Colton standing in the doorway. "I couldn't stand being around all those people anymore. I needed to be alone."

He reached down to take her hand, but she denied him. "Don't—Colton, did you hear that phone ringing in the service? How disrespectful. Don't people have enough sense to turn on a freaking phone at a funeral?"

"I'm sure it was an accident."

"Of course, you'd feel that way. You might as well leave now. There's no reason to stay."

"What's going on, Harini? You've been shutting me out since our son died. I'm grieving, too. I love that baby as much as you do."

"Colton, you wanted an out…" she responded, "now you have one. You should be happy."

"You're upset right now."

"I have every reason to be upset. All I have in my head is that chapel room at the funeral home—the organ music, the director and his staff walking around with blank expressions on their faces. The smells, Colton… too much perfume and cologne mixed with the scent of burning candles and fresh flowers. It all reminds me of death. That my baby is dead."

"I hate seeing you like this," he said. "You shouldn't be alone."

"Colton, I know about the job offer in Dallas. You're not in love with me. Just take the job. Besides, you deserve to be with someone who isn't defective."

"I don't want to leave you like this."

"Pip will be home for a while. I won't be alone."

"I need to know something, Harini."

"What?"

"Did you seduce me because you wanted to have a child?"

"I care for you, Colton. I won't lie—I wanted a baby with you, too. I thought that one day you and I might make a great team, but I was wrong. You still love Bailey. Maybe this is why our baby died. Because of what we did to her. We're being punished."

"Don't think that way, Harini."

"It's true. God knows I'll be a bad parent so that's why he keeps taking my children."

"You know Bailey well enough to know that she'd never let me back into her life after what we did to her. Besides, she left town."

Harini was surprised by the news. "When did this happen?"

"She left a couple of weeks after everything went down."

"How do you know this?"

"I ran into a friend of hers. After telling me off, Maurie let me know that Bailey moved back home."

Harini's grief was too strong to revel in this small victory. All she cared about was the painful truth that she would never be a mother.

"You really want me to leave?" Colton asked her later, after everyone was gone. The only people in the house with them was Pip and he was downstairs in the living room.

"I know you want that job in Dallas. It's perfect for you."

"I'm glad Pip ended his vacation early to attend his nephew's funeral and to be here with you."

Harini followed him downstairs in silence.

After Colton left, she walked over to the lone figure standing near the fireplace. "Thank you for being here."

He smiled. "Where else would I be? I'm your brother."

"Don't get cute," Harini sniped. "You can be on your way. I don't need you anymore."

Wordlessly, he held out his hand.

She handed him a check, then opened the front door. "Goodnight."

Harini sank to the floor in loud sobs when she was alone. It wasn't fair that she'd had to suffer such a grievous loss—to be robbed of motherhood. To be robbed of a man to love her. What was the point in having money and success if she ended up alone?

Chapter 16

Harini tossed and turned all night long. She kept wondering if losing her children were the repercussions of all she'd done? *This is not what I wanted to happen. All I ever wanted was to be successful. That means being number one—being the best.*

She got up and walked down the hall to the nursery.

"Sis, you need your rest."

She turned around to find Pip standing in the doorway. "I can't sleep. I just don't understand why this keeps happening to me. Why can't I be a mother?" She broke into sobs.

"You are a mother," he murmured. "You had three children. They are with the Lord."

"I want my children to live. I want them alive and well. I *deserve* to be a mother. All these skanks walking around popping out babies like candy…" Harini wiped her face with the back of her hands. "I'm never going to be able to have a child. Not ever."

"Why don't we have some tea?" Pip suggested.

She nodded.

"Those children… had they lived, they would've been

lucky kids with you for a mom. You would've been great at mothering, and it would've made you very happy."

"Nothing would have made me happier," Harini murmured. She would have made sure that all her children felt loved. They would know how proud she was of them. A lone tear rolled down her cheek. Harini placed a hand to her stomach, then burst into loud sobs.

After a cup of lavender tea, she felt a calm wash over her as the rain, gently tapped against the window. "I used to sleep through the night when it rained like this. It was so peaceful."

Pip nodded in agreement.

"I don't feel that peace now. All I feel is pain and disappointment. I actually thought Colton would insist on staying but he didn't. He's leaving town to take a job in Dallas."

"There wasn't ever going to be a you and him, sis. I know that you wanted more from Colton, but you knew going into this affair that his heart belonged to another woman."

"Bailey is not going to want him back." Harini wiped her face with her hand. "I would've been good to him—Colton just wouldn't give me a real chance."

"You cared for him," Pip said.

"I still do," Harini responded. "I was falling in love with him."

"It never would've worked out, sis."

"You don't know this for sure."

"You know it. You could never be completely honest with Colton."

Harini knew Pip spoke the truth. With a sigh, she pushed away from the table and rose to her feet. "I'm going to bed. Hopefully, I'll be able to sleep through the rest of the night."

"I'll see you in the morning."

She entered her room and climbed into the king-sized bed. Harini felt alone—truly alone. There was no one to share her life with. Her expensive bed felt cold and empty—just like her womb.

BAILEY SAT at the kitchen table, sipping a cup of coffee. Dawn was just beginning to break over the horizon. She had been up for a couple of hours thinking about Trace and how much he'd come to mean to her.

She and Trace laughed a lot. They shared the same sense of humor which she found very sexy. There was something about shared laughter that created a special kind of intimacy between two people. He got her, and Bailey got him.

Shortly after eight a.m., her doorbell rang.

"Who in the world is here at this ungodly hour?"

Bailey was surprised to see Trace at her door. "Good morning."

He smiled. "I thought I'd bring you and your mother breakfast."

"Perfect timing," she responded. "I was just going through my refrigerator trying to figure out what to cook."

Trace followed Bailey into the kitchen.

"So, what did you bring?" she asked.

"I picked up some southwestern omelets and fresh fruit from Michele's restaurant. I remember you saying that your mother loved their omelets."

Smiling, Bailey said, "You're going to make her day."

"I was wondering who had the courage to come knocking at the door this early," her mother said.

"Trace brought breakfast, Mama," Bailey announced. "It's your favorite from Michele's restaurant."

"Praise the Lord," her mother said. "I was craving one of those omelets. I guess the Lord heard me."

The three of them sat down at the table.

Bailey stared at him, this handsome man who had invaded her life. The man who had restored her laughter, had shown her that she could still have a life and had become her inspiration to write again. What Bailey felt now was a fragile, tentative hope that she hadn't felt for months... hope that she could one day get back to writing, and it was all due to Trace. It was at that moment Bailey realized that despite her every intention to the contrary, she was falling in love with him.

After her breakup with Colton, Bailey wasn't sure she would ever be able to trust another man, but she felt differently about Trace. They were kindred spirits. It wasn't hard to trust him. It wasn't hard to love him—Bailey only had to allow him into her heart.

HARINI BURIED her child a week ago.

"Are you feeling any better?" Pip inquired when he found her standing near the fireplace.

"I'm numb," Harini responded.

"Maybe you shouldn't have sent Colton away. He could've helped you through this."

She shook her head. "Trust me, I didn't have much of a choice. I gave him an out and he took it." Harini's eyes welled with unshed tears. "Like you said, it was never going to work between us. I'm just glad he can't go back to Bailey. I can't stand seeing her win."

"I hate seeing you this way."

"It's not fair, Pip, but there's nothing I can do about it. It's gonna take time, but I'll get through this heartache. I always do. For now, I need to get myself together so that I can focus on my writing. It's the only thing I have left."

"I'll leave you to it," Pip said. "I'm here if you need me, sis."

"I know. I'll be fine."

Alone in her office, thoughts of Bailey entered her mind. Harini was sure her nemesis would be jumping for joy over her painful circumstances. She was sure that Colton had already reached out to let her know he was a free man.

I know she won't take him back, but it still hurts because Colton made it clear that he didn't love me.

Harini was used to winning. It bothered her that Bailey still had Colton's heart. *But I have the book and my story is coming out.* She kept vigil over the social media outlets, but nothing from Bailey had come through. In fact, it looked as if she had closed all of her accounts.

The idea that Bailey had run away like a timid rabbit thrilled her. She was a great writer and would've been fierce competition for her, but Harini wasn't about to let that happen. She would be number 1 at all costs. She had worked too hard to settle for less.

She wasn't in the mood to write anything, so she just sat at her desk and stared out the window.

AFTER DATING FOR TWO YEARS, Trace and Bailey said their I do's during a beachfront ceremony in Wilmington on the first day of July. There were no more shadows across her heart and trusting him came easy. She was finally able to lay the past to rest.

Bailey and Trace made the rounds at their wedding reception, greeting everyone in attendance.

"Your mother is trying to get your attention," she whispered in his ear. "You better go see what she wants."

"I'll be right back."

Cassidy hugged her. "I'm so happy for you. You and Trace make such a beautiful couple."

Maurie embraced her next. "Welcome to the family."

Bailey grinned. "This is the happiest day of my life. Can y'all believe it? *I'm married*."

The trio burst into laughter.

"It's so good to have the old Bailey back."

"Cass, this is the *new* Bailey. I'm definitely not the same person."

"How is your mother doing?" Maurie inquired. "She looks pretty in that purple gown."

"She's having a good day, thank the Lord," Bailey responded. Her mother had suffered a stroke six months earlier. "She doesn't have any major issues with her hand. It's gotten so much stronger. Life is good for all of us."

"That's wonderful," Cass said.

The music started playing.

"Let's party," Bailey said. "I need to find my husband, so we can have that first dance."

"You do that," Maurie said with a chuckle.

On the dance floor, Trace pulled Bailey into his arms, drawing her close. He pressed his lips to hers, settling for a chaste kiss, instead of the lingering, passionate one they both desired.

His eyes traveled down the length of her, nodding in obvious approval. "You look so beautiful, sweetheart."

Bailey held up her left hand to show off the nearly two-carat emerald-cut engagement ring with its platinum matching band. "This is truly the happiest day of my life—becoming your wife."

They were soon joined on the dance floor by family and friends. Bailey and her new husband danced into the beginning of their new life together.

ON THEIR FIRST WEDDING ANNIVERSARY, Bailey welcomed Trace home to a candlelit dinner.

He presented her with a beautiful bouquet of red roses and a gorgeous tennis bracelet. "Happy Anniversary."

"I have something for you as well. Bailey handed him a gift.

He unwrapped the gift and opened the box to find a custom card with the miniature pink and blue pacifiers attached, then his gaze traveled to her. "Is this… are you…"

Bailey nodded. "We're having a baby."

A grin spread across his face. "I'm going to be a daddy."

"You are," she confirmed. For as long as she lived, Bailey didn't think she would ever forget the look of pure joy on his face when she told him about the baby she was carrying.

"This is the best gift you could've ever given me." Trace got up and walked over to where she sat. "I love you, sweetheart. More than you will ever know."

His declaration rang in her heart, in her very soul. She felt his love washing over her, through her. Bailey kissed him. "I love you, too."

"I can't believe we're having a baby. I know we talked about starting a family. I just didn't expect it to happen this soon."

"Neither did I," Bailey said. "I thought I had a stomach flu until I realized that I was late. That's when I took the pregnancy test. I saw my doctor this morning and she confirmed it. We're pregnant."

Trace stood, leaned over Bailey and placed his lips over hers. He brushed a light kiss across her forehead. "I want you to know that you're my dream come true, sweetheart. The answer to a prayer."

"You're so good to me, Trace. My life can only get better from this moment on. In fact, I have another surprise for you," Bailey announced. "I've started writing again. A book. At least, I think it's going to be a book."

"That's wonderful. Have you considered joining a writer's group?"

"I'm not ready for something like that," Bailey answered. "I'm not comfortable sharing my work with anyone else."

"Well, I'm glad you're writing again."

"Me, too. To be honest, I really missed it. The stories haven't stopped coming. I have so many—it was hard trying to decide which one to write first."

"So, do you have a title yet?" Trace inquired.

"No," Bailey responded, "but I'm really excited about this story."

He chuckled. "I can tell."

"Hopefully, I'll have it finished by the time the baby comes. Then I can shop it around while I'm on maternity leave."

"I'd like for you to think about leaving your job," Trace said. "This will allow you to be home with our child and write full-time."

"Really? You wouldn't mind?" This was more than Bailey ever expected. She wanted nothing more than to be a full-time writer and mother. The timing was perfect. Bailey was burnt-out with working claims.

"Not at all. I would prefer it."

Bailey kissed him. "You really are the best husband a woman could want."

"I hope you'll always feel this way."

"As long as there are no secrets between us—we're good," Bailey said. "I don't like hidden agendas."

Chapter 17

June 2018

"We're so happy to have the bestselling author of Black Rain, Bailey Hargrove with us tonight to discuss her new book, Seasons..."

Smiling, Bailey strolled confidently through the crowd, turned right, and headed toward the podium. A couple of flashes exploded, sending purplish spots flashing across her eyes. She turned to face the sea of people who had come to the bookstore to meet her. She never expected to find the bookstore filled to capacity. Seeing so many people there for her, thrilled Bailey beyond words.

When her first book came out last year, Bailey drew a decent crowd, but it paled in comparison to her signing now. Her eyes traveled to Trace, who was taking photographs of the readers in the audience who'd ventured out to see her.

Bailey read a passage from Seasons. When she was done, the room erupted in applause. "Thank you," she murmured. "I hope y'all will enjoy taking this journey with Elyse." Her gaze traveled the length of the area. "Are there any questions for me?"

She briefly recalled Harini mentioning how much she hated book signings. Bailey had been shocked by the admission. It was the opposite for her. Bailey loved meeting her readers. *If it weren't for them, I wouldn't be standing here now.*

After Q & A, Bailey sat down to autograph copies of her books. It thrilled her whenever someone walked up with both Black Rain and Seasons. She was proud of her literary babies.

"Did I tell you how beautiful you look tonight?" Trace questioned when they were in the car and headed to the hotel. "I'm so proud of you."

"Ten years ago, I never thought I'd get here," Bailey said. "I'd pretty much given up."

He inclined his head, asking, "Does it still bother you? What happened?"

"At times," she admitted. "I think what hurts most is that I thought she was my friend. I trusted and admired Harini…"

"At some point you two are going to run into each other."

"I know," Bailey said. "It's one of the reasons I didn't attend a lot of literary events—in the beginning. I didn't want to be anywhere near Harini, but now I think we can actually co-exist. I don't have to talk to her."

"I thought you said you'd forgiven her."

Bailey shifted her position in her seat. "I have, Trace. I just don't want to have anything to do with Harini. I've eliminated all the toxic people in my life—this includes her."

He nodded in understanding. "It's foul what this woman did to you. I know you feel helpless."

"Harini basically colored within the lines. You can't copyright an idea."

"She actually thinks that it's okay to do something like that to someone you call a friend?"

"Trace, that's just it. She was never my friend," Bailey responded. "She didn't care anything about me. She had an agenda from the moment I met her—I was just a pawn."

Bailey shrugged in nonchalance. "It was a valuable lesson. I won't ever be that naïve again." She leaned against him and wrapped an arm around him. "Why don't we change the subject? I want to celebrate."

"Unfortunately, I have to head to the airport to catch a flight. When you were signing books, I received a call from the hospital. One of my patients has been admitted. I've already booked my flight home."

"I'll ride to airport with you."

"No, the driver's going to drop you off first, then take me," said Trace. "I know you're tired, so get some rest. You've got a busy week ahead of you."

When the car pulled in front of the hotel, Bailey kissed her husband. "Thank you for coming with me, Trace."

"Enjoy the rest of your book tour. I'll see you when you get home."

Bailey walked him to the door. "Give Maddie and T.J. a kiss from me. I'm missing them like crazy already."

Since leaving Philadelphia in 2008, she'd met and married a wonderful man; given birth to two beautiful children and was now a published author. Bailey couldn't ask for anything more —her life was just as she always wanted. Her stomach rumbled, reminding her that she hadn't eaten since early afternoon. She'd been too nervous about the signing.

In the hotel, Bailey perused the room service menu, then called and placed her order.

While waiting for her food to arrive, Bailey's thoughts centered on Harini. She'd heard from Cassidy that the child conceived with Colton had died. At that time in her life, Bailey had not been able to summon up any sympathy for the woman, but now she felt differently, having suffered her own miscarriage six months ago.

She and Trace decided to wait another six months before trying to conceive again.

Delayed but not denied, Bailey thought as her gaze bounced around the luxurious hotel room. She finally had the life as a successful author that she'd dreamed about, and she had a loving husband and two adorable children. Harini, on the other hand, was alone. Her relationship with Colton hadn't lasted long at all. Bailey had no idea whether her singleness was a personal choice or not, but there were times when she detected a glimpse of loneliness in her eyes whenever she was caught on camera unguarded.

"It's inevitable. I will see you again," Bailey whispered. "Only this time I won't be the same woman."

Bailey threw herself on the bed. She felt herself sinking deliciously into it. It was like resting on a cloud.

She rolled completely over and off the other side and opened the door to the bathroom. Its shining white porcelain and tiles gleamed at Bailey. She gazed admiringly at the tub, which was sunk into the floor.

Tentatively Bailey touched its sides. Smooth.

Turkish towels were on the rack. She moved quickly and picked one up. It was light and soft and fluffy. She buried her face in it. It wasn't coarse like the cotton towels.

She took a deep breath. This was luxury.

She climbed inside and leaned back in the tub lazily, a delicious languor seeping through her. The water was covered with sparkling exploding bubbles, and their perfume hung heavily in the air. Slowly she stirred, running her hands down over her body.

Bailey could feel her flesh soften in the water. She pulled a towel from the rack beside the tub and wadded it into a small pillow. Carefully she placed it on the edge of the tub and leaned back on it to keep her hair from getting wet. Bailey closed her eyes.

This felt so good.

So good.

The next day, Bailey stood outside the hotel and looked down at Broadway. Despite the morning hour, the streets were already crowded. Everybody was going somewhere. People had intent, serious faces and never once stopped to look around. She'd enjoyed New York City.

Thirty minutes later, she was headed to the airport.

Her next stop, Philadelphia.

"I SEE Bailey Hargrove's new book is out," Pip announced. "Her first one did really well, and it's been optioned for a movie. Are you planning to attend her signing tonight?"

"No," Harini responded dryly. "I have no intentions of watching Bailey flaunt her success in my face."

"You didn't think we'd ever hear from her again, but I knew better." Pip glanced over at her. "How is your new book coming along?"

She sent a sharp glare in his direction. "You know how it's doing."

"Looks like sales are just okay? I wonder why…"

Harini's body stiffened in her chair. "Pip, what did you say?"

"You know if you'd stay off of social media picking fights with everyone—you might actually come up with a solid story-line. But you're too nosy to stay off the Internet. You are always looking for dirt on folk—it's how you get off. It's starting to affect your sales. Readers don't want to read about authors beefing with each other. Truth be told—it's a turn-off."

"I don't agree. If that were true, then reality shows wouldn't be so popular now," Harini countered. "Besides, they should know the truth about some of these people."

"Then start with yourself," Pip challenged. "Tell your readers the truth."

"You might be my brother, but I don't have a problem kicking you out of my life. You are either with me or against me."

"Ooooh... I'm so scared..." He eyed Harini. "What's got you in such a mood? I know it's not just because Bailey's in town."

"Bailey and I were both nominated for best in fiction by Book Times Magazine," Harini announced. "I just saw that she won."

"How do you feel about it, sis?"

"That I deserved it more. I've been nominated every year for the past ten years and I've won each time. However, a lot of my so-called sister scribes have complained that these awards are just a popularity contest. I think Bailey won just to shut them up. The magazine needs subscribers and a lot of authors vocalized that they would no longer support it."

"You read her book. What did you think of it?"

"It's alright. I don't see what the fuss is all about," Harini responded.

"Can you ever say anything nice about any other author's books?" Pip questioned. "Because I can't remember the last kind word you've said about someone else's work."

"This is why I hate talking to you sometimes."

Pip shrugged. "Too bad. You're stuck with me."

Harini stormed out of her office, muttering a string of profanity.

"Was it something I said?" Pip called out after her.

AFTER THE PHILADELPHIA SIGNING, Bailey sat down to dinner with Cassidy and Maurie. This was her first time back in Philadelphia since leaving to return home to Raleigh.

"Girl, it's so good to see you," Cassidy greeted as the two

women embraced. "The last time I saw you was at your wedding."

"I know," Bailey responded. "I promise to do better. Helping my mom, settling into my marriage and being a mother has kept me busy… then my writing…"

"I'm so proud of you," Maurie interjected.

Bailey hugged her next. "I'm so glad y'all are here with me. I've really missed you both."

Maurie took a sip of her drink. "You look happy."

"I am," she responded. "Trace is a wonderful husband and father. My children are my everything. My writing career is fantastic—I have no reason to complain."

"It's well deserved," Cassidy said.

The waiter arrived with a tray of entrees for them.

"The bookstore was crowded," Maurie stated before slicing off a piece of fish and sticking it into her mouth.

Bailey smiled. "I always wonder if I'm going to walk into a store with only ten people waiting to see me—I tell myself that if I do—I'm still going to have fun."

Cassidy leaned forward in her chair. "So, tell me how it feels to have a movie adaptation of your book?"

"It's incredible," Bailey said with a grin. "Right now, we are in the script writing phase of this journey."

"I thought Harini might show up," Cassidy said. "Even if only to try and upstage you."

"I didn't expect to see her." Bailey took a sip of water. "I don't think she's woman enough to face me one on one."

Maurie agreed. "She wouldn't chance a one-on-one confrontation in public like that."

"I would never confront Harini in front of readers," Bailey stated. "If and when I do have a talk with her… it will just be the two of us."

"Bailey, is it even worth it? Look at you… success is the best revenge. You're a bestselling author; you have a great marriage and two children. What does Harini really have outside of her books? A cold bed? The heartbreak of losing her baby?"

"You're right, Cass. It's not that I want to live in the past." Bailey shifted her position in her seat. "I just need to tell her exactly how I feel about what she did to me. Who knows? She might be doing the same thing to someone else."

Maurie wiped her mouth on a napkin. "Enough about Harini. Let's talk about something more important. *Dessert.*"

BAILEY WAS LOOKING FORWARD to seeing Dallas. *I wish I had enough time to visit the Arts District. Maybe Trace and I can come back before the year is out.*

Since the success of her debut novel, Black Rain, Bailey felt as if she'd hit the floor running. Her publishers were happy and had just offered her a new contract with a six-figure advance. Her career had really taken off, for which Bailey couldn't be happier.

She was grateful.

Her painful experience with Harini was in the past. Bailey intended to leave it there. She refused to look backward.

Bailey knew Colton lived in Dallas, but she hadn't really expected to see him at her signing. Especially with the way things ended between them.

She kept her eyes from lingering on him too long as they landed on everyone in attendance.

Bailey was a little surprised that he'd waited around until she'd autographed everyone's books and stock copies. When he approached the table, she stood up and greeted him with a polite smile. "Colton... it's nice of you to come." The animosity she once felt for him was gone.

"Congratulations. I always knew you had it in you."

"Thank you." She picked up her purse and headed toward the exit doors.

"Bailey, I took a chance of coming here tonight because I wanted to talk to you."

Her expression blank, she eyed him. "About what?"

"Can we grab something to eat?" he asked. "Please…"

"We can go to the restaurant on the corner," Bailey responded after a brief pause.

Once they were seated, Colton blurted, "I'm so sorry for my part in what happened.

You didn't deserve what I did to you."

"It's all in the past," she said. "We've both moved on. I have a wonderful husband, two children. A six-year-old girl and a boy who's four."

"That's good to hear. I actually got married four years ago." Colton shifted uncomfortably in his seat.

Bailey smiled. "I'm very happy for you."

"I'm a father now, too. I have a son. He's three years old."

She was genuinely thrilled for Colton. "You have to show me pictures."

After giving the waitress their drink orders, they pulled out photographs of their children.

"I'm glad you were able to bounce back after what Harini did to you—what *we* did to you."

"Back then, I don't know which hurt worse. Your betrayal or hers." Bailey took a sip of her water. "But like I said, it's all in the past, so it really doesn't matter anymore."

"Can you forgive me?" Colton asked.

Bailey smiled. "I forgave you a long time ago. I've forgiven Harini, too." She paused a moment before saying, "I do want to know one thing. Did you love her?"

Colton shook his head no. "To be honest, there was something not quite right with Harini—I couldn't fully trust her."

Bailey couldn't resist asking, "What do you mean?"

"She was just weird about some things. Harini never wanted to talk about her past. I thought it was strange that she didn't have any family pictures anywhere in her place."

"Her brother lived with her—at least that's what she told me."

"I talked to the man a few times on the telephone, but I never met him face-to-face until the day she left the hospital. Apparently, he travels a lot. Pip was always sending postcards and texting photos."

"Wow… that's interesting. So, you didn't really get to know him."

"Harini lost the baby a couple of months after everything went down. I landed a job here in Dallas, so I left Philly. As painful as it was to lose my child, it's worked to my good."

Their food arrived.

"When you were in Philly, did you see Harini?" Colton inquired. "I'm hoping she had the good sense to apologize to you."

"No, but I will see her eventually," Bailey responded. "The literary circle isn't that big. We are bound to run into each other. As for an apology, I'm not expecting one and it's fine. I'm so over her."

"Bailey, there's something you should know about Harini," Colton said. "Deep down, she's a very insecure woman. She puts on this act like she's got it all together and that nothing bothers her, but it's just a façade."

"I find that a bit surprising. According to Harini—she's the next best thing to Jesus."

"You are a fantastic writer, and don't you ever forget it, Bailey. Harini knew it and that's why you became a threat. Just know that you're now an even bigger threat to her now because you're in the same league. She plays dirty."

Bailey shrugged in nonchalant. "I'm not afraid of Harini Samuels."

"It's good to see you doing well," Colton said. "I wish nothing but the best for you. I want you to know that—it's all I ever wanted."

"Thank you," Bailey responded. "I wish the same for you."

When she left Colton at the restaurant—Bailey left her past with him where it belonged. In the past.

Harini—she was a different story.

Back at her hotel, Bailey showered, slipped into a pair of pajamas, then climbed into bed.

She called her husband. "Hey you…"

"How was the signing? Trace asked.

"It went well. Did you check on Mama? Make sure she's taking all of her meds."

"She's fine, sweetheart. She told me to tell you not to worry so much."

Bailey chuckled. "How are my babies

"Finally asleep," Trace responded. "They both miss you. T.J. kept asking when you were coming home. I told him that you'd be home soon."

"I miss all of you." Bailey paused a moment, then said, "I saw Colton. He came to the signing."

"Did you two get a chance to talk?"

"Yes. We went to dinner. He apologized for everything. He's married now and has a son. I told him about you and the children. Colton's happy and so am I. It was nice."

"So, you were able to get closure."

"Yes," Bailey responded. "I think it was the same for Colton, too."

"Sounds like you've made peace with your past," Trace stated. "I'm glad."

"Me, too." She picked up a pillow and held it close to her. "I can't wait to come home. I really miss you."

"Our bed is lonely without you in it."

Bailey talked to Trace until her eyelids grew heavy. "I'm

getting sleepy. I'll call you tomorrow when I get to New Orleans."

"I love you, sweetheart."

"I love you, too."

She ended the call, then rearranged the pillows for her comfort. Bailey pulled the covers to her chin, reveling in the softness of the comforter. "I'm so loving my life right now," she murmured.

Chapter 18

"Bailey Hargrove's book is number 1 on the *USA Today* best-sellers list," Kaile announced when she ran into Harini, who happened to be signing stock at a bookstore in the Galleria. "I can only imagine how much it must thrill you to see your former protégé doing so well. Speaking of which, why didn't you attend her signing on Tuesday? It was packed in there—standing room only,"

"Of course. I'm very happy for her," Harini responded sardonically. "I noticed I didn't see your book *anywhere* on the list."

"And neither was yours," Kaile countered. "Looks like her book sales are much better than ours. I think it's wonderful."

Harini did not respond.

"When I talked to Bailey, she mentioned that this was the fourth book she's written. I asked her whatever happened with that first one. I recall her being very excited about it."

Harini glared at Kaile. "And what did she say?"

"Oh, I'm sure you already know. You were her *mentor* at the time."

"We parted ways. She was too married to her work."

Kaile burst into laughter. "Same ole Harini…" She turned and walked away, still laughing.

Harini was fuming by the time she arrived home.

"What's got you in such a mood?" Pip asked.

"I saw Kaile. That witch has always been jealous of me," Harini answered. "She wants to try and humiliate me; well, what few readers she has is about to find out that she's nothing more than a homewrecker. I don't think they're gonna stick with her when they find out she's messing around with a married man. That's who paid off her bills and bought her that house."

"You sure you want to do this?" Pip asked, following Harini to her office. "I thought you'd stopped blasting people on social media."

"I need to put Ms. Jefferson in her place for trying to bait me. Bailey didn't tell her anything because if she had—I know Kaile wouldn't keep it to herself. She'd take great pleasure in ruining me." Harini sat down at her desk.

"You two have a lot in common," he responded.

"I'm nothing like *her*."

"You and Kaile both like to keep drama going." Pip shook his head. "It's so immature."

"She can't handle the fact that I'm the top bestselling African American author. She's never been number one, and the truth is that she's not good enough."

"Right now, Bailey's the one topping all the bestseller lists."

"That won't last long," Harini uttered. "I'll make sure of that."

"Why can't you get it in that head of yours that there is room for every author? There's no need for competition."

Harini broke into a harsh laugh. "I know you can't really believe that nonsense. The literary world is saturated with people calling themselves authors. Half of them can't write—it makes the rest of us look bad."

"Instead of criticizing, why don't you do something to help them if you really feel this way?"

"I've tried," Harini responded.

"Then you need to do a better job," Pip told her.

"Leave me alone," she uttered.

"I'm out."

She watched her brother storm out of her office, then turned on her computer. "Everybody is about to find out what a slut you are, Kaile Jefferson." Using her secondary social media account, Harini posted photos of Kaile and her married lover, rapper Zeke.

BAILEY HAD ENJOYED MEETING her readers, but when her plane landed at the Raleigh-Durham Airport, she was thrilled to be home. She missed her husband and as much as she had enjoyed staying in luxury hotels—she looked forward to sleeping in her own bed.

Trace was parked at the curb when Bailey walked out with her luggage. He got out of the SUV and embraced his wife.

"I missed you, sweetheart."

"I missed you, too."

She settled into the passenger seat while Trace stuck her travel tote and suitcase into the back of the vehicle.

"I know you're tired, but I want to make one stop before we go home," Trace announced when he entered the SUV. "It's on the way."

"That's fine."

When he turned into a neighborhood of gorgeous expen-sive-looking homes, Bailey assumed he was making a house call.

He came to a stop in front of a house with a *For Sale* sign in the yard.

"What are we doing here?"

"I wanted you to see this house. We talked about buying..."

"It's beautiful, honey, but I think this may be a bit out of our price range."

"The owner is very motivated to sell."

Trace parked, and they got out of the vehicle.

They were met on the porch by the realtor.

As soon as she stepped in the grand foyer, Bailey found the home warm and inviting.

"I want you to see this room first," Trace said.

Double doors opened to an elegant library, surrounded by custom built-ins, a coffered ceiling, and sleek Brazilian cherry flooring. Bailey and Trace moved forward while their realtor stayed near the entrance.

"This is so beautiful," Bailey murmured. "It's the perfect place to write. *I love it.*"

"I thought you would say that," Trace said.

They proceeded to tour the rest of the house.

"Formal living, formal dining," Bailey murmured as she noted the architectural custom details throughout. "I love the size of this family room. Especially the stone fireplace. I can just visualize Maddie and T.J. camped out in here watching television."

"What do you think of the kitchen?" asked Trace.

"I'm in love." Bailey's gaze traveled from the high-end stainless-steel appliances to the large central island to the spacious breakfast area which opened to a gorgeous bright sunroom. "There's a bedroom with private bath on this floor— I was thinking it could be for your mom."

"That would be perfect."

They went upstairs.

"There's four bedrooms on this level, each with its own bath," the realtor said.

Bailey walked into the master suite. "Oh, my goodness. This is gorgeous."

"It's ours if we want it."

She glanced up at her husband. "Really?"

He nodded.

"I put in an offer last week and it was accepted. This is our new house."

A smile lit Bailey's face. "Oh, my... I can't believe we're going to be living here. What do we need to do now?"

Trace laughed. "We should probably go home and start packing."

Inside the car, Bailey said, "I'm sitting here trying not to pinch myself."

"This is all real, sweetheart."

"All my dreams have come true, Trace. "I have you, Maddie and T.J.—my mama and I are closer than we've ever been; I'm published and now we're moving into this beautiful house. There's nothing else I want—I have everything."

Trace leaned over her and placed his lips over hers. The kiss began soft and tender and grew in intensity until it held all the desire, all the love he felt for her. And with the emotions she tasted in his kiss, Bailey believed in him, in their love, but most importantly, she believed in herself.

THE NEXT MORNING, Bailey turned onto Peach Briar Avenue, her Nikes striking the pavement with an even thud. Sunlight blurred her vision, so she reduced her pace for the last stretch of her five-mile run, regulating her breath for the slow-down, and glanced at her watch.

A trickle of sweat slid from Bailey's temple down to her jaw, and she brushed it away with her hand. Her mind was clear, energized by her run.

It was eight-thirty a.m. As soon as she made it home, Bailey intended to jump into the shower, then settle down to write. She enjoyed being able to focus completely on her craft. With her mother moving into the new house with them, the kids wouldn't have to be shuffled from their home whenever Bailey had to travel.

"I didn't expect you to still be here," she told her husband seated at the counter when she walked into the kitchen.

"I'm making our plans for Aruba. How long do you want to stay?" Trace glanced up from the laptop.

"Let's see… I'm thinking two weeks of sun and sand. Some tennis. How does that sound?"

He smiled. "Sounds good to me."

Bailey eyed him in disbelief. "Really? Two weeks. You're going to take that much time off from work?"

"Yes. I want to enjoy my family. We're taking your mom with us, so we can have some quality time."

"You've already spoken to her about it?"

Trace nodded. "She's excited about going."

"Mama's always wanted to go there," Bailey said. "So, have I."

"I think we should leave the weekend after we close on the house," he suggested.

"Let me look at my calendar, but I'm thinking it'll work." Bailey began to dance. "We're going to Aruba…"

Trace burst into laughter. "I need to get out of here. Call me after you check your schedule, sweetheart. I want to book our tickets today."

She walked over to him and kissed his cheek. "Love you."

Bailey watched him stroll toward the door leading out to the garage. *I'm so lucky*, she thought. *I have everything I want except one thing.*

Revenge.

THAT AFTERNOON, Bailey worked on her new book until the kids came home.

"How was your day, Maddie?" she asked her daughter after planting a kiss on her cheek.

"Sara told me that she's not my friend anymore."

"Oh no… did she say why?"

"I wouldn't give her my ham and cheese sandwich." Maddie plopped down on the sofa beside her mother. "I didn't want her peanut butter sandwich so I wouldn't trade."

Bailey bit back a chuckle. "I have an idea. Why don't I make an extra sandwich for you tomorrow. You can give one to Sara."

"Yes. Then she'll be my friend again."

Bailey called out for her son. "Hey… where did you go?"

"I went to see Nana. I wanted to give her a hug."

"Well, where's my hug, sweetie?"

He rushed over to her. "Right here, Mommy."

Bailey reveled in his embrace. She loved being a mother. "How was your day?"

"Gooder than yesterday," T.J. responded. "My teacher was sick and we had another one—she was so mean."

"Today was better because your teacher came back today."

He nodded.

Bailey spent the better of an hour with her children, helping them with their homework. She looked forward to moments like this, which is why she always attempted to write while they were in school. Family time was very important to her.

HARINI OPENED her door to find an irate Kaile standing there. "How did you get past my doorman?"

"I know you're behind all the lies going around on social media."

"Don't get mad at me because the streets are talking," Harini responded. "You shouldn't be messing around with a married man—that's on you."

"You're a seriously vile person. Zeke has nothing to do with this—why did you involve him?"

"Because apparently you're nothing more than a home-wrecker." Harini gestured toward the door. "Get out and don't come back to my place without an invitation."

"One day…" Kaile uttered. "You just wait… your time is coming."

Harini laughed. "I hear Zeke's wife posted several not-so-nice tweets about you."

"You better be glad I don't feel like going to jail today."

"You should be thanking me for not posting the mug shot when you got arrested for prostitution. You go around here acting like you so sweet and innocent—but people don't know the real you, Kaile. By the way, does Zeke know that you were once a hooker?"

"You know what I've been through, Harini. I shared those things with you because I thought you were my friend." Shaking her head, Kaile added, "I was so stupid to ever trust a snake like you."

Harini shrugged.

"Did I tell you that Bailey showed me pictures of her children. They're so cute and adorable. She mentioned that she and her husband were planning on having another baby. Wonderful news, don't you think?"

Her words punched Harini in the gut.

"Bailey looked really happy. She has a handsome husband… two children, and two books that are doing great—

all the things you wanted. You shared some stuff with me, too. *Remember*. I bet that big expensive bed of yours is as cold as a coffin."

Fighting back tears, Harini screamed, "*Get out of my house*." She opened the front door. "If you want a fight—I'll give you one, Kaile."

"I better not see another thing on social media about me and Zeke or my past," she warned. "I promise I'll make your life miserable. You see... I know a little something about you and a certain author with the initials R.S."

Harini's surprise was evident, but she tried to keep her expression bland. "I don't know what you're talking about."

Kaile walked through the open door. "Remember what I said..."

Harini folded her arms across her chest as if to ward off a chill. *How could she know?*

How could she have found out? She'd been so careful.

"What's done in darkness will always come to the light, sis."

She turned around to face her brother who was standing at the entrance of the foyer. "Kaile wouldn't hesitate to expose me. She's just fishing."

"Whatever helps you sleep at night," Pip responded.

Chapter 19

"How's work coming along?" Bailey asked. She decided to call and touch base with Cassidy while she ate lunch. Normally she would eat with her mother, but JoAnn had plans with some of her friends from church.

"Nothing's changed here. Oh, except that Beth finally made manager."

Seated at the counter, Bailey said, "That's wonderful. She'll be a good one."

"She always asks about you."

Bailey smiled. "I really liked her. She was about the only person on my team I was close to—she cried when I put in my notice."

"Have you seen all that stuff on social media about Zeke and Kaile?" Cassidy inquired.

Bailey responded, "Yeah, I have." She glanced out the window in her office. "I feel terrible for her."

"I don't condone infidelity, but I feel bad for Kaile, too—it's her personal business out there like that."

"I'm pretty sure Harini is the one who did this," Bailey said. "She and Kaile used to be close. I don't know what happened between them, but they're no longer friends. She's the only person I know messy enough to do something like this."

"Wow... she really is a piece of work... that woman."

Bailey nodded in agreement. "She is that..."

"Maurie and I are taking the kids to a festival this weekend. You should see Zoey and Legacy together. They're hilarious."

"Madison always asks about them," Bailey said. "T.J. talks about your son a lot. He calls him *the friend*. He's always asking, when am I gonna see the friend?"

Cassidy chuckled. "Joey wants to move to North Carolina, so he can hang out with T.J."

"I think that's a great idea," Bailey said.

"Girl, Joe is not leaving his job to start over down there," Cassidy stated. "He'd lose seniority if we transfer. Trust me, I already broached the subject with him. Anyway, how's your writing coming along?"

"Great," Bailey replied. "I'm actually thinking of revisiting the first book I wrote."

"I hope you do. I really loved that story. But why now?"

"I'm finally in the space to deal with that part of my past, Cass."

"Have you seen Harini?"

"No, but that day is coming," Bailey said, "and I'm looking forward to it."

FROM THE MOMENT they arrived in Aruba a couple of days ago, Bailey felt as if she'd stepped into a piece of heaven. The Renaissance Resort Hotel near downtown had its own island where pink flamingos and iguanas roamed freely.

While her mother and the children were having breakfast, Bailey and Trace enjoyed a couple's massage in a cabana.

Afterward, the entire family enjoyed a day at the beach.

Bailey and Madison built a sandcastle while Trace and T.J. played near the water's edge.

Her mother and the kids settled into their suite after an early dinner, so that Trace and Bailey could enjoy the evening as a couple.

"Aruba is everything I thought it would be," Bailey said.

They were able to secure beach chairs in front of the Moomba bar to watch the sunset which was painted in beautiful shades of orange, yellow, red, and pink.

"I love it here."

Trace placed an arm around her. "So, do I."

Later in the evening, Bailey and Trace decided to do as the Arubans do and drive up to the California Lighthouse. She'd read that it was the perfect place to enjoy the magnificent skyline of the most northern tip of the island.

The stars were bright and shining and the moon hung heavy in the sky. The faint roar of the surf came to her ears and a warm, soft breeze came from the ocean.

"This is so perfect," Bailey said. She reached over and took Trace's hand in her own. "I've dreamed of traveling the world with the man I loved since I was a little girl. My dad used to tell me that I should be grateful for the simple things in life and I am. But I never saw anything wrong with wanting more."

"You're right," Trace responded. "There isn't anything wrong with that. I'm happy that I get to see the world with you."

"I almost let my dreams die when I left Philadelphia." Bailey shook her head. "I won't let that happen again."

"Am I imagining this or are you still very angry with that woman—the one you said betrayed you?"

"It's not anger really," Bailey said. "I'm just not going to let her forget what she did to me. I promised her that she would one day pay—I intend to see that she does."

"Do you think this is healthy?"

"I guess you don't," Bailey responded. "You asked, and I gave you my truth. Maybe one day I won't feel this way, but for now, maybe we should change the subject."

"You won't get an argument from me."

Bailey lovingly touched his cheek. "Why don't we go dancing? We can have a couple of glasses of wine, then party the night away." She didn't want thoughts of Harini to put a damper on their time together in Aruba.

A WEEK after their vacation ended, Bailey attended the Virginia Literary Festival in Richmond. She was thrilled to have her mother, the children and Trace with her. While they were out sightseeing, Bailey went to check in with the conference coordinator.

She ran into Kaile at the registration table.

"Hey Bailey, it's good to see you."

"You, too."

Kaile's eyes bounced around their surroundings. "I see the gossip mill is still running amuck," she said, shrugging. "It's a good thing I really don't care what people think of me. Besides, Zeke and I have been over for a long time."

"Did you ever find out who leaked it?" Bailey inquired.

"You and I both know who is behind this." Kaile waved her hand in dismissal. "Speaking of the witch, she just arrived."

Bailey's eyes followed her gaze to where Harini was standing. They locked eyes for a moment.

She was pleased when Harini looked away first.

Bailey and Kaile walked passed her without speaking.

"I hope you don't mind my asking, but what happened between you and Harini?" Kaile inquired. "I know something must have taken place because the two of you were so close, then you went ghost. I couldn't even find you on any of the social media platforms."

Bailey was silent for a minute, debating whether to tell Kaile the truth. She decided to be honest. "Harini had an affair with my ex-boyfriend—only he wasn't an ex at the time."

"That last child she lost? Was that his baby?"

Bailey nodded. "Yes."

"Oh wow… I wasn't expecting that." Kaile shook her head in dismay. "I'm so sorry."

"It's fine. The truth is that Harini couldn't have gotten pregnant without Colton's help. He is just as much to blame for what happened, if not more. But it really doesn't matter anymore. I'm married to the man I'm supposed to be with."

"I guess that was enough to make you leave town."

"That wasn't the only reason, Kaile." Bailey glanced over her shoulder to see if anyone could hear what they were discussing. She turned back to face Kaile and said, "Not only did she have an affair with Colton—she also took my storyline and sold it as her own."

Bailey eyed the woman sitting across from her. "You don't look surprised."

"Unfortunately, I'm not."

"Did she do that to you?"

Kaile shook her head. "She knew better than to try something like that with me. However, I've heard other writers say this about Harini recently."

"Are you serious?"

"Yeah. There are a couple of people here I'd like you to meet," Kaile said. "I need to speak with them first though."

"That's fine."

"Harini is taking advantage of a lot of folks. She's not loyal —not even to her friends… if she still has any."

"One day she's going to get what's coming to her," Bailey stated. "Trust me on that."

"Have you ever read any books by Randy Spook?" Kaile inquired.

Bailey shook her head no. "Why?"

"He only had two books come out before he died. He was only twenty years old and a fantastic writer. You should check him out."

"Oh wow… what happened to him?"

"I think he had a heart attack or something. If you read his books, I'm sure you're going to find them very interesting."

Bailey wondered why Kaile was being so cryptic. "You know something, don't you?"

"Not really, but I have a theory. There's a connection between Randy and Harini. Read his books and tell me what you think."

BAILEY SEARCHED out Kaile at the welcome reception.

"Hey, I was just about to come looking for you. I want to introduce you to Lanelle Chase and Mariah Sanderson."

"It's nice to meet you both," Bailey said with a smile.

"They're both writers," Kaile announced. "And Lanelle is actually from your area."

"You live in Raleigh?"

Lanelle nodded. "Yes. I have to tell you that I loved both Black Rain and Seasons."

Mariah interjected, "Seasons was my favorite."

"Another thing you all have in common is that at one point, Harini was your mentor," Kaile interjected.

Her words were met with silence.

Smiling, Kaile said, "I thought you ladies should meet."

She glanced over her shoulder. "My agent's here. I'm having dinner with her, so I'll see you in the morning."

Bailey gestured toward a nearby table. "Shall we have a seat?"

"So, Harini was once your mentor, too?" Mariah inquired.

"It was a long time ago," Bailey responded. "Ten years to be exact."

Lanelle played with her napkin. "Her mentorship ended when I found out that she wasn't at all who I thought she was."

"Same here," Mariah said. "I have to say I was very disappointed in the way things turned out. Harini was supposed to be helping me with me book—the next thing I knew... she had a book coming out with the same storyline."

"Did the same thing to me," Lanelle said.

"Oh wow..."

"What was your experience like with Harini?" Lanelle asked.

"Sadly, it's the same as yours," Bailey answered. "But she didn't just take my idea—she also got pregnant by the man I was dating at the time. That's what hurt the most at the time. There are just certain boundaries friends shouldn't cross, but then... Harini really wasn't my friend."

Lanelle shook her head in disbelief. "Now that's really messed up."

"I fault him because Harini didn't hold a gun to his head." Bailey paused a moment before continuing. "I stopped writing because of what happened. Because of what she did to me. But then I met my husband and he's the reason I'm even published. He really helped me regain my confidence."

Lanelle smiled. "That's nice. It's good that you have someone in your life who is so supportive."

"How did you get over what she did to you?" Mariah bit into a soft taco.

"Time," Bailey responded. "It's took a while, but I was finally able to move pass what happened."

"Well, I'm not over it," Lanelle stated when Mariah left the table to talk to another conference attendee. "I want Harini to pay for what's she's doing. Mariah and the other girls are afraid of her. They worry that she'd black ball them or expose them in some way."

"You're not worried?" Bailey wanted to know. "You see what she's done to Kaile and other authors."

Lanelle shrugged. "I'm not scared of Harini Samuels. Let her come for me. Besides she doesn't have anything on me. I keep my personal life private."

Bailey nodded in agreement. "My sentiments exactly."

"Does that mean that you'll join me by exposing people like her who prey on new writers?"

Bailey smiled. "Definitely. There's no telling how many we don't know about. We just have to wait for the right opportunity. We have to be smart in the way we handle this situation."

Lanelle agreed. "You're right. Taking this to social media will not make us any better than Harini—she's into the public shaming. What we need to do is educate writers so that they are aware that piranhas like her exist in the world."

"Exactly," Bailey said. She felt the tiny hairs on the back of her neck stand up. She glanced over her shoulder and found Harini staring. Bailey met her gaze with a hard stare of her own. *You don't scare me.*

As if she'd read Bailey's thoughts, Harini looked away.

Satisfied, she turned her attention back to Lanelle. "Let's get together one day next week," Bailey suggested.

"I'd love that."

Bailey glanced back over to where Harini was standing. *I'm coming for you.*

Chapter 20

Harini took the elevator to the floor she was staying on. She couldn't erase the smug expression on Bailey's face out of her mind.

Watching her first with Kaile and now Lanelle… she knew Bailey was up to something.

There's nothing you can do to me. You don't have anything on me. All you can do is whisper about me, but you're not woman enough to face me. None of you.

She walked over to the window in her suite and looked out.

Harini saw Bailey walking hand in hand with a tall handsome man. A woman holding the hands of two small children followed close behind. She'd heard her family was with her but hadn't seen them before now.

A flash of anger and grief washed over Harini. Why did Bailey deserve to have a family while she was alone? Why couldn't she have her heart's desire?

She continued to watch them.

There was something familiar about the man, Harini thought. She was able to get a better look when they were under the street light. She searched her memory but could come up with nothing.

"I know I've seen this man somewhere. I'll figure it out," she whispered to the empty room. "I've got to find something to use against Bailey."

BAILEY PURCHASED the two books authored by Randy Spook. She couldn't wait to delve into them. She tried to get Kaile to share her theory, but to no avail. Bailey was curious as to what connection Harini could have to this author.

She left the book store, then headed to meet Lanelle at a restaurant located in the next block.

"I had a great time at the conference," Lanelle said as soon as they were seated. "The highlight for me was meeting you."

"That's sweet of you to say," Bailey responded. "I enjoyed myself as well. They had some interesting workshops. I really liked the one on Arson. I have an idea for a mystery and the handouts the facilitator gave out is helpful."

"The Southern Writer's Conference coordinator invited me to do a workshop at their conference in Orlando. I would like you to be a part of it," Lanelle stated. "Especially since Harini is going to receive a Lifetime Achievement Award at the awards banquet."

"Really?"

"Our workshop can be on mentoring."

"I like that idea," Bailey said. "But we have to make sure we keep it professional, Lanelle. We can't ambush her."

"Even though that's what she deserves."

"Look, I want revenge too."

Her mother entered the room with two glasses of lemonade. "I thought you two might need something cool to drink."

Bailey smiled as she accepted a glass. "Thanks Mama."

"Thank you," Lanelle said.

When they were alone, she asked, "How many children do you have?"

"Two," Bailey responded. "I have a daughter, Madison and a son. His name is Trace, but we call him TJ."

Lanelle almost choked on her drink.

"Are you okay?" Bailey asked.

"Yes, I'm sorry. I think the lemonade went down the wrong pipe or something." Lanelle wiped her mouth with a napkin. "Trace. That's an unusual name."

"He's named after his father," Bailey stated. "I do agree that it's not a common name you hear a lot."

"So, what does he do? Your hubby?"

"He's a psychiatrist."

"You married a doctor," Lanelle said with a tight smile. "That was my mother's dream for me, but it didn't work out that way."

"If you don't mind him working long hours and being on call… don't get me wrong, Trace is a great husband and father, but there are times when it seems like we're two ships passing in the night. However, he should be arriving home soon."

Lanelle checked her watch. "Wow… I didn't realize the time. I really need to get going. I have a deadline looming and I'm behind with my writing."

"Call me when you get a free moment to discuss this workshop we're doing." Bailey walked her to the door before navigating to the kitchen to grab a bottle of water.

She heard the front door open and close.

"Trace is that you?"

"Yep."

He strolled into the kitchen. "Who was that I just saw leaving here?"

"Lanelle," Bailey said, "She and I are going to be on a

panel together at the Southern Writer's Conference in Orlando on mentoring."

"How do you know her?"

"She's the one of the authors I told you about—Harini took advantage of her as well. That's why we're doing this workshop—so that other writers are aware that some people are not to be trusted in this industry."

"You're sure you want to do this?" he asked.

"Why not?" Bailey inquired. "It's not like I'm going to put her on blast."

"You have to know she's going to come after you," Trace said. "From everything you've told me, she's vindictive."

"Let the witch come. I may not be able to sue her, but Lanelle and I can at least prove that she's a snake. The same way she finds dirt on people—I'm sure there are some major skeletons in her closet. I just haven't bothered to look until now."

"So, you want to hurt her back? You want revenge?"

"Don't you think I deserve it?" Bailey asked. "Trace, there are times when you have to call people on their mess. All I'm doing is firing a warning shot. I don't want Harini going around hurting innocent people. It has to end."

"Sweetheart, vengeance belongs to the Lord. When are you going to give this over to Him?"

"I've waited ten years for God to do something about her. I'm tired of seeing Harini get blessing after blessing when she's such a horrible person."

"Sweetheart, the Bible clearly tells us how Jesus taught that many of His blessings fall upon all people regardless of their behavior or response toward Him."

"I know that," Bailey uttered. "Matthew 5:45 says, for he makes his sun rise on the evil and on the good and sends rain on the just and on the unjust. I still don't think it's fair."

"Don't forget that we often only see the good that happens

to bad people rather than the entire situation. We don't see both the blessings and struggles. Besides, those blessings are only limited to this life. Remember the story of the rich man and Lazarus?"

Bailey nodded. "My father used to preach a sermon on how the rich man was asking for help in his torment and was reminded that the good things took place during his life on earth while Lazarus lived in suffering. My dad used to say that God's children will enjoy eternal joy while those who are in the world will experience eternal separation from Him."

"You believe that, don't you?" Trace questioned. "The ultimate blessing of living in God's presence for eternity should outweigh any situation that appears unfair or unjust in this world."

"What about all those people Harini's hurt?"

"You can't save the world, Bailey. You can encourage those that are hurting, but I don't think you need to stoop to that woman's level. That's what you'll be doing."

"We're just going to have to agree to disagree, Trace. I'm not going to vilify Harini publicly, but I'm also not going to keep quiet about my experience—it could help someone else."

"I'M GETTING A LIFETIME ACHIEVEMENT AWARD," Harini told her brother. "It's about time someone recognized my efforts," she stated. "I should have several of these by now."

"You should really be more appreciative. After all, you're only thirty-six years old. You have a lifetime to garner more awards."

"Pip, I'm grateful. I appreciate it, but you know that I deserved one of these years ago."

He walked over to the window and stared out. "Why do

you think you're the only person in the world who should get everything they want?"

"How can you say that? I don't get everything I want," Harini responded. "I've been denied children, a husband... I didn't do anything to deserve this. My one prayer has never been answered."

"Are you trying to blame God for what's happened in your life?"

"He controls all," Harini stated.

"You made certain decisions, sis. Not all of them good."

"Isn't that why we have grace?"

"I'm not doing this with you today. Congratulations on your award."

"Pip... why can't you just be happy for me?"

"I'm sure you already know the answer to your question."

"You can be so hateful at times."

"Apparently, it runs in our bloodline," Pip responded. "The same can be said for you and most of our family."

"Are you still mad at our father? I don't understand why? You know that he thought the world of you. I was the failure. I was just average, and Pip, you know he and Mother considered *average people* beneath them."

"Father was very judgmental, but I'm not angry with anyone. I let that go years ago."

Their home culture did not include unconditional love toward the children—Pip was idealized while she was devalued. Excessive value was placed on status and achievement. Their parents were not empathetic people, instead shame and public humiliation were used to teach obedience. Harini was frequently compared to Pip and told, "You should be more like your brother."

"I could never be you," she murmured. "They hated me for it."

"Our parents weren't perfect, sis. They had their own

issues, but that's all in the past. You are in control of your life now."

"I often wondered if they really loved each other," Harini said. "They used to argue a lot. I can still hear Mother saying, you don't care about me. You're too busy feeding your perverted obsession with those naïve little nurses who treat you like a God."

"I would put my pillow over my head to block out her screaming," Pip confessed. "Father was always so calm. He'd tell her, "Charlotte, it's late. Let's not fight.""

Harini agreed. "That would make Mother even angrier."

"Father slept downstairs on the sofa most nights," Pip responded. "I can only remember a few times that they actually slept in the same bed."

"Mother once accused him of ruining her life. I never understood why she would say something like that."

"She married our father because she was pregnant, sis. I'm not sure she loved him, but she wasn't the type of woman who would raise a child alone—much less twins." Pip paused a moment, then said, "There's something you didn't know about our mother."

"What's that?"

"Mother used to threaten suicide when she didn't get her way. Father always thought it was a ploy for attention, but when she actually followed through on one of those threats— he stopped keeping certain medications in the house."

"She tried to kill herself?"

Pip nodded. "Don't you remember when she was in the hospital for almost two weeks?"

Harini searched her memory. "That's right... Father said that she'd had a mental breakdown. He was so humiliated. That's why he wanted to resign from the hospital and move up north."

"We pleaded to stay in Georgia. Mother came home and

after that—she didn't complain or argue with him anymore. She became the perfect wife in a loveless marriage. Apparently outward appearances meant more to her and Father than her own happiness."

"To leave him would've been the ultimate shame," Harini said. "I would probably feel the same way. I felt that way when Colton walked out on me. I'm so glad I never told anyone about us."

"Being happy has always been more important to me," Pip stated.

"But it's gotten you nowhere."

He burst into laughter. "That's where you're wrong, sis. I lived every single minute of my life. I'm happy and nothing will ever change that—not even you." Pip headed toward the office door. "Try to enjoy this journey. You've certainly done all you could to get here."

Harini clenched her fist. Her brother could be such a pain at times.

Chapter 21

"Harini doesn't deserve an award like that. Kaile is more deserving—she's actually helped other authors—not taken advantage of them."

"Lanelle, I agree, but we have to stick to our plan," Bailey reminded her. "We can't make it sound like it's jealousy or sour grapes. We give our talk and let the audience ask the questions. We then speak our truths without naming names."

"That works for me," Lanelle said.

They talked a few minutes more before ending the phone conversation.

T.J. and Madison was in school, so Bailey picked up the first book written by Randy Spook and began to read. She'd finished the first draft of her new book and needed some time away from it before starting the next round of revisions.

By the end of the first chapter, Bailey whispered, "Wow…" The story was engaging and had drawn her in from the very beginning, but it was the style in which Randy wrote that caught her attention.

Kaile was right about there being a connection between Harini and Randy. Bailey just couldn't figure out the details.

She continued to read.

One thing for sure. Bailey wanted to learn more about the late Randy Spook.

"I CAN'T BELIEVE you're leaving me tomorrow for four whole days," Trace said.

Bailey walked out of the bathroom wearing a robe. "You're going to miss me, huh?"

"You know I am." He embraced her.

Bailey stepped away from Trace. "We're going to be late for our dinner reservation if you don't let me get dressed," she warned. "Why don't you check on the kids? I'll be down in a few minutes."

He laughed. "I know what you're doing."

"I'm kicking you out, so I can put some clothes on. I'm hungry. After you feed me, then we can come back here, and you can ravish me all night long."

Trace openly admired the strapless black dress that fit as if it were made just for her body when Bailey came downstairs.

"You look beautiful."

"And you are as handsome as ever," Bailey responded. She retrieved a coat from the downstairs closet and put it on.

He escorted her to the car, and then opened the door to the passenger side.

She climbed inside the SUV.

Trace walked around to the driver side and got in.

Soon they were on their way.

They chose a restaurant in the downtown Raleigh area for their date night.

"I feel like I haven't had a chance to sit down and have a real conversation with you in almost a week."

"This class I'm teaching is almost over," Trace said. "After this semester, I can resign."

"No, I don't want you to do that, Bailey said. "I know how much you love to teach. I would never ask you to give that up. We just have to have more date nights."

He smiled. "You won't get any complaints out of me."

Their food arrived.

Bailey sampled her grilled chicken entrée. "This is delicious."

Trace sliced off a piece of his steak and stuck it in his mouth.

"How is it?" She asked.

"Good," he responded. "You know sweetheart... have you thought about teaching creative writing classes?"

Bailey shook her head. "It's not for me. I'm a writer and it's all I want to do—just write my books. That's enough to keep me busy."

"One way you can put what you've been through behind you is mentoring someone. You're worried about those other writers. Become a mentor."

"No," she responded. "I don't want that responsibility. I mean it. I simply want to write—not swim around in what may be a polluted pool."

"That's where you are most needed, sweetheart. Be the example of a true mentor."

Bailey wiped her mouth. "This is our date night. No more talk about work."

When they returned home, she and Trace retreated straight to their bedroom where she kissed him hungrily, her curves molding to the contours of his body.

"Bailey..." Without finishing the thought, Trace picked her up and carried her over to the bed.

HARINI LIFTED her eyes from the book in front of her and rubbed them wearily. They felt red and raw and burning. She looked out the window.

It was still snowing.

She was looking forward to spending the rest of the week in Orlando, Florida. It would be a warm reprieve from the wintry weather in Philadelphia.

She stared up at the sky. It was still snowing heavily.

"Can't sleep?"

Harini turned around to face her brother. "I didn't hear you come in. What are you doing up at this hour?"

"You know I've always been a night owl."

"Why couldn't I please our parents?" she asked.

"You were a child. They had their own problems, sis."

"I needed them just like you did, Pip."

"I actually believe that you needed them more than I did," he responded. "It was just a difficult time."

"Mother was so consumed with making sure we looked like the perfect family to everyone. I think that's the real reason we started going to the church."

"I don't know if that's true. I think she was overwhelmed. She'd become a mother relatively young." Pip shrugged. "I don't know…"

"I met Reggie a month after I moved here. My writing took off and after a few months, so did he. He never knew about the baby. I was in so much pain at that time. Then Mother and Father died. That's when you showed up." Harini smiled. "I was so happy to see you. I didn't know how much I needed you until then."

"So, here we are on the cold winter night."

"Here we are…"

Chapter 22

Bailey and Lanelle arrived in Orlando on Thursday morning.

"According to the agenda, our workshop is today at 11 a.m. We have time to get to the hotel and freshen up."

"This is my first workshop," Bailey confessed. "I was up late practicing last night."

Lanelle chuckled. "You're going to be fine."

The first person Bailey saw when she walked through the lobby was Harini who said, "I was surprised when I saw your name as one of the presenters. Two books and now you think you're an expert." She broke into a harsh laugh.

"I don't claim to be an expert by any means, Harini. That's what you do. My workshop is on finding the right mentor. Are you being catty because you're worried about what I might say?"

Harini slithered close to her. "You'd like that, wouldn't you? One thing for sure. I've never been worried about you, Bailey."

They locked gazes. "That was your first mistake."

Lanelle walked over to where they were standing. "Well isn't it the great lady herself… Harini Samuels."

"How interesting that the two of you have suddenly become besties." While pretending to admire her nails, she added, "I guess it's to be expected. After all, you two have a lot of *shared* interests."

Bailey rolled her eyes heavenward before saying, "I do hope you're planning to attend our workshop, Harini. I'd love to hear your thoughts on it."

"If I don't have a better offer, then I just might stop in."

"We look forward to seeing you then," Lanelle said. "It's not like you have a line of folks waiting to talk to you."

Bailey stifled a laugh as they strode off leaving Harini with an ugly scowl on her face.

"That wasn't very nice, Lanelle."

"She deserved it."

Bailey glanced at her watch. "We need to get to the Emerald room. We have like ten minutes before our session starts.

"You think Harini's going to come?" Lanelle asked.

"Oh yeah," Bailey murmured. "She's not going to miss this for the world."

After a brief introduction, Bailey said, "Whether you're a novice writer looking for answers to basic questions or a frequently published one with years of experience under your belt, every writer can benefit from having a mentor. But where do you find the right mentor?"

Her eyes traveled to the woman who'd just entered the room. Bailey bit back a smile. She knew Harini wouldn't be able to resist coming to the workshop—she was both curious and just straight nosy.

Lanelle spoke next on the several ways a writer could benefit from mentorship. While she talked, Bailey's gaze darted back and forth to Harini.

Fifteen minutes before the end of the workshop, they opened it up for questions.

A young writer raised her hand, then stood up. "I'm a new writer and I came up with what I think is the perfect title for my book, but then a book came out earlier this year with that same title. Can I still use it?"

"Yes, you can," Bailey responded. "You can't copyright a title."

"Thank you."

Another person stood up. "My question is pretty much the same except I was in a critique group and one of the people there used my title for their book. I have a problem with it."

"I can understand why you'd feel that way," Bailey said. "While what that person did is not illegal, this becomes an issue of morals." Her eyes traveled to Harini.

Their gazes met and held.

"I agree with Bailey," Lanelle interjected. "I experienced exactly what you mentioned but it wasn't just my title. I thought this person was my friend. I thought she wanted to help me. Instead, my outline became her next book."

A sea of murmurs swept across the room.

"I experienced the same thing," Bailey interjected. "As you can imagine, the sting of betrayal was painful. I stopped writing for four years. I am still not comfortable discussing any of my ideas with anyone other than my agent and editor."

"Unlike Bailey, I didn't let what happened stop me from writing. I was angry, but I let that anger fuel my determination to make it as an author. Like Bailey, I don't talk about my work with other writers."

"So, there isn't anything a person can do legally when this happens?" the writer in the audience asked.

"I'm afraid not," Bailey responded. "The way that I made it through was to come to the realization that what God has for me is for *me*. Nobody can tell my story the way I can.

Nobody can tell your story the way *you* can. Just hold onto that." She could feel the heat of Harini's glare, but Bailey didn't care. This was only the beginning of what Harini would have to face.

"Would either of you ever consider another mentor?" Someone from the audience asked.

"I would," Lanelle responded. "I know that all people aren't the same. It's just that I'm being very careful this time around. I'm going to really get to know the person instead of believing in the hype."

"Like Lanelle said, I'll have to take my time. I'll ask more questions. We listed some questions you ask when looking for a mentor—not just for your writing career. You can use these for work as well. One thing I want to say is that the person who did this to me—that person will have to answer for it. Not to me, but to God. As I said before, what God has for me—it's for me. I allowed that person to delay my calling, but they couldn't stop it. That was just one idea... I have so many more—more than I can ever write." Bailey smiled. "Keep writing."

WHISPERS SURROUNDED Harini as she sat in the audience listening to Bailey and Lanelle play the victim.

She caught a few people giving her subtle glimpses, but she ignored them. No one was brave enough to accuse her directly.

They didn't dare.

Besides, she hadn't done anything wrong. Harini sighed in frustration. She was sick of writers not understanding how it worked in the publishing industry. There were only so many freaking plots in the world. It's not like she'd plagiarized their work. They could still put out their work—it didn't resemble anything she had written. *Just get over it already*.

After the workshop, Kaile walked over, a grin on her face. "It's a shame what some people are doing; taking advantage of writers under the guise of helping them. I can't image who could be so cruel."

"Get away from me," Harini hissed.

"You know... I heard several people whispering that they thought it was you, but I said to myself... naw... she's self-absorbed, petty and messy... but she isn't low down enough to steal other people's ideas."

Harini moved closer to Kaile saying, "You sure you want to have this dance with me? I haven't done anything wrong, but you... you have a lot to hide, don't you? Like how you were arrested for harassing Zeke's wife a couple of months ago."

Kaile's surprise was evident.

"Oh, you didn't think I knew about that." Harini smiled. "I *know* everything."

"I really don't know why I should be shocked? This is what you do. Look for dirt on everybody. You just don't bother to find out the whole story. Zeke's wife confronted me and when I wouldn't back down, she called the police and accused me of harassing her. You need to stop what you're doing, Harini," Kaile warned. "People are talking about you. Rumors are already swirling."

"As if you care anything about me."

"I don't," Kaile stated. "I don't like anything about you. I'm just making sure you understand that the first shot's been fired. You're going to mess with the wrong person and they won't care about exposing you."

Lifting her chin, Harini said, "I'm not worried about that."

"I don't believe that for a minute. I saw your face. You were terrified, especially when Bailey was speaking. I saw her look directly at you."

"Was it the same look I saw on yours when I mentioned your arrest?"

Kaile slipped the strap of her purse on her shoulder. "You

can erase that smug expression. You haven't won yet. Just know that I'm not the one you're going to have to worry about. Bailey Hargrove is a different story."

Harini walked out of the conference room.

She caught sight of a group of authors staring at her. Harini lifted her chin, stared ahead and walked toward the elevators.

Once she was in her hotel suite, Harini picked up a pillow and tossed it across the room. "I'm not about to let you two skanks get away with this." She was getting a Lifetime Achievement award on Saturday night, but Bailey and Lanelle were trying to ruin it for her.

She paced the floor, fighting back tears.

Harini picked up her cell phone, then tossed it on the sofa. She put a fist to her mouth, muffling her scream.

"I THINK THAT WENT WELL," Lanelle said when they settled in Bailey's hotel room.

"Did you see that look she gave us?"

"Girl… she wanted to choke the life out of us."

Laughing, Bailey agreed. "Harini was *hawt*. I have to confess that it felt good seeing her squirm."

Lanelle picked up a pillow on the sofa. "I don't know if you noticed, but people started looking at her and whispering. I think they knew that it was her."

Bailey shrugged in nonchalance. "She deserves more than that as far as I'm concerned."

"I'm really glad Kaile introduced us. I really admire you and I hope that we become great friends."

Touched, Bailey said, "Lanelle, that's so sweet of you to say."

"I mean it. After what I experienced with Harini—I truly

appreciate women like you and Kaile. You're both comfortable in your success and you don't mind sharing information or lending support. This is real girl power." Lanelle paused a moment, then continued. "Bailey, I'd like for you to think about being my mentor. I completely understand if you don't want to do it. I just want you to please think about it."

"Oh wow…"

"I hope I didn't just make things awkward between us."

"You didn't," Bailey responded. "For the most part, I want to just stay in my lane and write, but I'll give it some thought, Lanelle."

"Thank you."

The conversation turned to relationships.

"So, are you involved with someone special?" Bailey inquired. "I couldn't help but notice that someone's been blowing up your phone."

"It's this guy. We've been dating for almost a year." Lanelle settled back against the sofa cushions. "He wants to take our relationship to the next level."

"What about you? How do you feel about it?"

"I don't think I'm ready for that. I have fun with this guy, but I'm not in love with him."

Bailey leaned forward. "Have you ever been in love?"

"Yeah. I have, but it was a long time ago."

"What happened?"

Lanelle took a long sip from her water bottle. "We were in college and things just fizzled out when he was in grad school."

"That's it?" Bailey asked.

She laughed. "Yeah. He was really focused on his career and I was obsessed with becoming his wife. When I realized what I was doing—I ended the relationship. He didn't object, so we went our separate ways. He's married now and here I am —still single."

"But you have someone who's crazy about you."

"You're right and he's not a psycho," Lanelle said with a short laugh. "Maybe I should go to my room and give him a call."

"I think you should," Bailey responded. "In fact, I'm going to give my hubby a call as well. I really miss him and my babies."

"How about we meet around six in the lobby for dinner with Kaile?"

Bailey picked up her phone. "I'll see you then."

Trace answered on the third ring. "Hello."

"Hey baby," she said in a sultry voice. "I miss you."

"I miss you, too. How did the workshop go?"

"Great, I think," Bailey responded. "Harini was in the audience."

"Really. How did that make you feel?"

"I wanted her there, Trace. I wanted her to hear everything Lanelle and I had to say."

"You wanted a reaction."

"I suppose so," Bailey responded. "I guess I just wanted Harini to know that it wasn't okay what she did to me."

"So, did you get what you wanted?"

"It's a start and please don't start lecturing me, Trace. I need to do this my way."

"Okay."

"Where's Maddie and T.J.? I'm surprised I don't hear them laughing and talking in the background."

"That's because they're in the kitchen with your mom. They're making peanut butter cookies for dessert."

"Fun times," Bailey murmured. "My sisters and I used to do that every Saturday night with her. We'd make cookies to give out after church on Sunday."

"They seem to be having a ball in there. Maddie rushed me out of the kitchen. She told me I had to stay in my office until dinner."

Bailey burst into laughter. "You're on a time-out. I love it."

After they hung up, she reached for her book. Bailey had finished Randy's debut novel and was in the middle of the second. She intended to finish it by the time she returned home.

Chapter 23

In a few short hours, she was to be on stage to receive a distinguished award. All attention was to be on her—Harini felt she deserved this recognition and the applause, but now it was tainted by rumors.

"I wish you were here, Pip so I wouldn't have to deal with this alone, but I'll be fine. I can handle these nobodies."

She felt a headache coming on. Harini lay down on the sofa, hoping it would ease off before the awards dinner. Since people were whispering about her—she needed to be the picture of perfection.

Once she was dressed, Harini eyed her reflection in the full-length mirror. She closed her eyes and raised her face as if to seek the warmth of a spotlight as the audience roared their love and appreciation for her. This is what she lived for—to be adored.

Tonight was to be no exception. From the beginning, she'd delivered on her promise of great stories. Harini felt she deserved to be recognized for her efforts.

Upon entering the ballroom, the first person she laid eyes

on was Bailey. She smiled as if she was the bearer of some great secret. Harini yearned to go over and knock the smug expression off her face but resisted the urge.

She took her seat and patiently waited for her moment to shine. Before the night was over, Harini would be acknowledged for her great body of work. This pleased her greatly.

Of course there were a few disgruntled authors in the audience, but she refused to let them steal her joy. She was the winner here and nothing could change that. The literary world was better with her being a part of it.

The time to accept her award arrived.

Harini rose up and walked gracefully to the stage. She smiled for the cameras as she accepted the beautiful statuette.

She had practiced her speech for days and it was perfect.

The only flaw in what would have been a wondrous and memorable moment was that there was no standing ovation—only applause.

She blamed Bailey and Lanelle.

They had ruined this evening for her and she was going to destroy them.

BAILEY WASN'T surprised when Lanelle sent her a screenshot of Harini's post.

"I agree. It's clearly directed at you," she told Lanelle over the phone. She low-key calling you a copycat."

"She can say whatever she want. I don't even know the person she's talking about and I didn't copy anything—the guy that did my website created my logo and everything." Lanelle chuckled. "She's ridiculous."

"We expected her to retaliate, so here it is—she's not finished though, so be prepared," Bailey said. "She doesn't have anything on me."

She really don't have anything on me either," Lanelle responded. "I guess she'll start posting bad reviews under fake names now."

They both laughed.

"Trace, I need to go to Georgia," Bailey told her husband when she got off the phone. It was time to go digging in Harini's closet.

He laid down the newspaper he'd been reading. "Why?"

"Research," Bailey responded as she joined him at the breakfast table. "I need to find out everything I can about Randy Spook."

"You're doing this for what?"

"I'm curious, Trace," Bailey said, "and I'm actually thinking of writing a book based on his life. He was an incredible writer who didn't get a chance to be what he could be. He's been dead almost 15 years. It would be nice If I could release this book on the anniversary of his death."

"I won't stop you, although I know this has more to do with Harini than anything else," Trace said, "but do what you have to do."

"I'm going to drive down on Thursday and I'll be back home on Sunday."

"I can come down on Friday," Trace offered.

"I'd love that. We could make it a romantic getaway."

"Then you'd better get all of your research out of the way before I get there."

Bailey gave him a sexy grin. "I intend to do just that."

Trace glanced down at his watch. "I need to get out of here. My first appointment is at nine-thirty."

"Do you want to meet for lunch?"

"Sure."

"Text me when you're able to go," Bailey said. "I know today is one of your busiest days."

"Let's plan to meet at the Mexican restaurant on the corner," Trace suggested. "Say one o'clock?"

"I'll see you then, sweetie."

He kissed her. "Have a productive day."

"Always," Bailey murmured.

She walked straight to her office and spent the rest of the morning searching for information on Randy Spook. Bailey jotted down what she thought might be relevant in her quest. *If I can prove what I believe—I've got you, Harini.*

BAILEY CHECKED into her hotel shortly after four on Thursday. The six-hour drive to Georgia was tiring. She unpacked, then settled down to relax and read over her notes. She knew that Randy grew up in River Oak, a small town outside of Atlanta.

Bailey went online to try and locate a copy of his obituary.

She nearly jumped for joy when she found it.

Randy leaves behind a sister Harriet. Another sister, Regina preceded him in death…

There wasn't much to it, but she now knew he had another sibling. She knew he and Regina were twins because he'd mentioned it in his dedication to her. However, there was another sister, although she could have passed on as well. "Harriet Spook… I hope I can locate you and that you'll be willing to tell me about your brother."

Bailey had not been able to find out any real information on the woman. No doubt she was probably married now with a family of her own. Hopefully, she was still in River Oak. If not, Bailey was sure she'd be able to find someone who knew the family.

She did another search to see if she could determine if Harini ever lived in Georgia.

There was no doubt in her mind that a connection existed between her and Randy. It was a puzzle Bailey was determined to put together.

She placed a quick call to Kaile.

"Hey, I have a question for you. Do you know if Harini ever lived in Georgia?"

"I don't think so. When we first met, I thought I detected an accent, but when I asked her about it—she kind of brushed it off. She told me she grew up in Maryland."

Bailey felt a thread of disappointment snake down her spine. "Oh…"

"Why do you ask?"

"I agree with your theory that there's a connection between Randy and Harini. When I was reading his books—I felt like I was reading one of her early books. Do you think that's why she's the way she is—maybe he did that to her."

"I'm not really buying that, Bailey. The voice and style of their books are eerily very similar. Every author has a unique voice. You may echo another writer, but there's still something authentic in your style of writing," Kaile stated. "I believe Harini used Randy's work as a guide for her first two books. I know it doesn't really make sense…"

"No, I get what you're saying. It's like taking a song by an artist and singing it the exact same way—not making it your own or adding your own unique spin on it." Bailey tapped her pen lightly on the desk as she talked. "If that's what she did, then why not keep it up? It was working for her."

"That's what I'm not understanding either," Kaile said. "The rest of her books are nothing like those first two books of hers. I figured she was trying something new, but when her sales went down, I thought she'd go back to the way she wrote her first two books, especially since she's obsessed with being on bestseller lists and winning awards."

"I don't have any answers for you, Kaile. Not right now,

but hopefully, I'll have some soon. I'm going to get to the bottom of this."

Chapter 24

Bailey eyed the photographs she'd just received.

Trace had flown down to Atlanta where she picked him up as planned. They spent a romantic weekend in Georgia, driving back home yesterday.

Shaken, she stared at the pictures once more, then tried to reach Trace on his cell, but the call went to voicemail.

Bailey called the office. "Hey, can I speak with my husband, Gina?"

"He's in a session. I'll have him call you when he's done."

"You know… don't worry about it. I'll just see him when he comes home."

Her next call was to Lanelle. "Can you meet me for lunch?"

"Sure."

Bailey vowed not to react until she talked to both her husband and her friend. The photographs were not recent, but an explanation necessary.

Lanelle arrived a few minutes after twelve. She took one look at Bailey's face and asked,

"Is everything okay?"

"Something's bothering me," she responded. "I'm sitting here trying to figure out why you never mentioned that you and my husband were once involved or better yet... why you never once revealed that you knew who he was."

Lanelle looked shocked. "It was a long time ago, Bailey."

"So why keep it a secret?"

"Did he tell you?"

"No, he didn't."

"Bailey, I really didn't know you were married to Trace when we met. I found out the first time you invited me over."

"But when you realized it—why didn't you say something?"

"You and I were becoming friends and I didn't want to lose that. I didn't think it would matter."

It bothered Bailey more that her husband never once mentioned that he had ever met Lanelle. It was a sore reminder of how Colton had betrayed her with Harini.

"He's the guy you were in love with, right?"

"Yeah," Lanelle answered, "It was a long time ago, Bailey."

"That's why I don't get all the secrecy," she stated. "Harini was able to find these photos of the two of you." She spread them on the table. "You look pretty cozy and very happy together."

Lanelle muttered a string of profanity.

"Trust is very important to me."

"Bailey, I didn't say anything because I didn't want it to be awkward whenever I'm around you and Trace."

"You should've told me."

"I disagree," Lanelle stated. "Your husband should have told you about our history."

"He should have," Bailey agreed. "And I'll deal with him about it. I'm curious. Have you talked to him recently?"

"Only once. I called him to see if he was going to say anything to you. I told him that I really liked you and I didn't want our history to ruin the friendship I was building with you."

Arms folded across her chest, Bailey eyed Lanelle. "So basically, you convinced my husband that it was a good idea to keep a secret from me."

"You know Trace… he has a mind of his own. He would've told you if he thought it was best, regardless of how I felt about it."

"I'm very disappointed, Lanelle."

"Bailey, I'm sorry. I wasn't trying to hurt you."

She could read the sincerity in Lanelle's eyes, but Bailey didn't like secrets. "Maybe not, but I still feel betrayed."

"And if you'd known… would we be friends right now?"

"I don't know," Bailey responded. "The point is I wasn't given the choice to decide on my own."

"You know who's behind this?"

"I do," Bailey said. "This reeks of Harini."

She heard the front door open and close.

"Good," Bailey uttered. "Trace is home. The three of us can finish this conversation."

"Hey sweetheart…" his voice died at the sight of Lanelle. "I didn't know you had company."

"I'm glad you're here. I'd like to hear from you why your past relationship with Lanelle was such a big secret." Bailey pointed to the photographs on the table. "You can thank Harini for exposing the truth."

"We weren't trying the deceive you in any way. I knew you were building a friendship with her—I didn't think it was a big deal. We broke up almost 15 years ago. It's ancient history."

"Somehow Harini found old pictures of you two and sent them to me to cause problems in our marriage. I need to know if there is anything else I should know? Any secret babies out there?"

"I honestly thought that a past relationship just wasn't worth mentioning," Trace told her.

"Would you still feel this way if I'd done this to you?" Bailey asked. "What if you were building a friendship with Colton? Wouldn't you want to know whether I ever dated him?"

"I guess if it was a relationship that truly meant something to you," Trace responded. "Do you want to know about all the women I've dated?"

"No, of course not."

"Lanelle and I discussed telling you, but she really liked you and she didn't want our history to be an issue. She wasn't trying to hurt you."

"I think I should leave and let you two talk," Lanelle interjected. "Bailey, I'm really sorry."

When they were alone, Trace said, "Sweetheart, I'm sorry for not being upfront about my relationship with Lanelle. In hindsight, I can understand why you're upset."

"Trace, the only reason why I haven't gone ballistic is because I trust you. I'm angry with you and Lanelle for keeping this from me, but I do understand that your intentions were good. But you know how Harini's going to make this look, don't you?" Bailey asked. "She's going to take this and run with it. Our personal life is going to be plastered all over social media."

"You know the truth, Bailey. That was a long time ago, and the truth is that she doesn't know that you're just finding out about my past."

"I am so tired of this woman."

"Don't let her get to you. She's not worth it."

"I know… I'm just sick of her going around here and ruining lives. At some point, Harini needs to pay for her sins."

"She will face the consequences of her actions."

"Yeah, you keep saying that, but all I see is Harini being

blessed with a new movie deal and more awards. Meanwhile authors out there are devastated and feel violated because of her."

"But she's alone," Trace pointed out. "That's all she has, Bailey."

"OH, WHAT DO WE HAVE HERE," Harini murmured when she saw the email from Bailey. "Pip, you have to hear this." She read the letter aloud.

> *Harini:*
>
> *I know you are behind the photographs I received. I'm sure this was an attempt to cause problems in my marriage and my friendship with Lanelle. I am writing to let you know that despite your best efforts—you failed because I already knew about their history.*
>
> *My marriage is stronger than ever, and Lanelle and I are great friends. Your attempt to wound me by sending old pictures of a time long past in my husband's life FAILED.*
>
> *I take solace in knowing that one day you will reap the consequences of your actions against others. You will pay for all you've done. I only hope that I will be around to witness your downfall. God has given you a real gift in your writing—yet, you choose to abuse your talent.*
>
> *I am warning you that if you persist in these attempts to wreak havoc in my life, I will have no choice but to go public with everything you have done to me. I will put you on "trial" publicly in the same manner as you have done with others. Your reputation is already stained.*
>
> *People are whispering behind your back. They are warning others to stay away from you. I'm sure you've noticed that your friendships are dwindling away—writers are no longer looking to be mentored by you. You will always have a few faithful stragglers, but for most—a plague is more preferable than being around you.*
>
> *Leave me alone. Do not contact me or send me anything. I am not*

afraid of you and have no problem digging through the skeletons in your closet. You have been warned.

Bailey

"The little cat has claws after all," Harini said with a chuckle.

"I told you she wasn't one to mess with."

"I'm not afraid of Bailey. There's nothing she can do to me." She burst into laughter. "Skeletons in my closet. Oh, she wishes…"

―――――

"YOU'RE sure you don't want me to go back with you to Georgia?"

Bailey shook her head. "You'd probably be bored. River Oak is really small and there's no Starbucks. I'm only going to be gone for a couple of days, Trace. I'll be back home before you get a chance to miss me."

"What are you hoping to find this time?"

"I don't know. I did get the name of a lady who used to work for the Spook family. I'm going to hear what she has to say and hopefully she can lead me to his sister."

"You really think this guy and Harini somehow knew each other?"

"I do. They had to cross paths at some point before he died."

"Maybe they didn't," Trace suggested. "Harini may have just come across Randy's books. She didn't need to meet him to copy his style of writing."

"I thought about that," Bailey responded. "But I can't explain it. I just feel that this goes deeper than anyone knows. Harini is very secretive when it comes to her life. Think about it—she brags about everything but is mum when it comes to her childhood… her past in general. The only thing I know about her is that she has a brother. That's it."

"You really didn't know her very long. Maybe it takes her a little longer to open up to people."

"She's hiding something, Trace. I trust my instincts."

Chapter 25

"Great morning to you," an old woman greeted when she opened the door to Bailey. "My daughter called and told me to expect you 'round this time."

"Thank you for seeing me, Mrs. Bennett."

"Folks 'round here call me Miss Clara Mae. I can't imagine why a famous author would come all the way to Georgia to talk to me."

"I wanted to speak to someone who knew Randy and his family. I heard that you worked for them."

"For a few years, but when I couldn't take no more of Charlotte Spook's attitude—I left. That woman vexed me more than a lil' bit."

"What can you tell me about them?" Bailey asked.

"When the Spook family came to town, we was all excited about having a black doctor, but he was so rude and stuck-up…" Clara Mae shook her head sadly. "They walked around town like they was stepping in high cotton while the rest of us was walking in dirt." Fanning herself, she continued. "Oh, they thought they was better than the rest of us. They had the biggest house on the largest acre of land... Dr. Spook was somethin' else, but his wife, she was even worse."

Bailey was enthralled as she listened.

"Charlotte kinda calmed down some after she had to go to Atlanta for a spell. I heard she had some sort of breakdown. Don't know for sho' but that's what people was saying. But when Randy got published... Lawd... you couldn't tell his mama nothin.' She pranced around town like a proud peacock in mating season."

"He was only twenty at the time," Bailey said. "I imagine she was very proud of him."

"We were all proud of Randy," Clara Mae responded. "It was nice to see something good happen for him. He spent a lot of time in the hospital."

"He was sickly?"

Clara Mae gave a slight nod. "They found out Randy had a bad heart when he was in high school. That's what killed him."

"I had no idea," Bailey said. "His sister Harriet—what can you tell me about her?"

"To the best of my knowledge," Clara Mae said, "Harriet's life was pretty much unremarkable which I'm sure disappointed her high falootin' parents."

"Is she still in the area?"

Clara Mae shook her head. "She left town after Randy died. I guess Harriet just couldn't bear to live in that house after what happened. No one had heard from her until she called my daughter a couple of weeks ago, and said she wanted to sell the house. Sharon told her that the place needed to be updated and it was in bad need of repair. Harriet instructed her to sell it as is."

"What happened to Randy's parents?"

"Dr. Spook and his wife died in a car accident about a year

after he passed away. Come to think of it—that was the only time Harriet came back to River Oak. She came down to bury her parents and close up the house."

"Why do you think Harriet wants to sell now?"

Clara Mae shook her head. "No idea. Guess she just wants to move on with her life. I thought it was mighty strange that she had an attorney handle everything for her. She only talked to my daughter that one time and told her to go through her lawyer for everything else."

"Were they close?" Bailey asked. "Harriet and Randy."

"I'd say so. Randy wasn't one for a lot of attention, but Harriet… she loved it. I used to watch the poor thing doing everything she could to get her parent's attention. Randy was their favorite and they didn't hide it. They showered the boy with love. Harriet… they ignored. One thing I remember about Harriet—she always had a book in her hand. That girl loved to read. If I had to pick, I woulda said she'd be the writer in the family."

"His twin Regina…"

"I'm afraid I don't know nothing about her. Heard she died when they was babies. They was still living up north then."

"Do you know where they're from? I had assumed that they lived in River Oak all of their lives."

"I think it was some place in Maryland."

Bailey glanced down at her notes. "I haven't been able to find any current pictures of her." Bailey said. "What did she look like?"

"She was a pretty girl—the way I remember…" Clara Mae appeared deep in thought. "You know there was something… Harriet had a birthmark on her left arm. It looked like a X or something." She pointed to a photo in an open magazine on her table. "Like this…"

Bailey stared down at the bottle of poison with a red X on

the label. She glanced down at her notes, then asked, "Randy died from his heart condition. So, there was never any suspicion of foul play?"

Clara Mae looked shocked. "Who'd want to kill Randy? He was a sweet kid and a gifted young man. He knew how to tell a story. Naw... poor thing... his heart just gave out. Why all this interest in Randy?" she asked. "You writing a book on his life?"

"I'd like to," Bailey responded. "He was a brilliant writer who died much too soon. Oh, I went by the cemetery, but there's no record of Randy being buried there."

"I heard a while back that Harriet had his body moved," Clara Mae said. "She was afraid fans would desecrate his grave, so no one knows where he's buried. I suspect she just wanted to keep him close by."

"Do you think I'll be able to see the family home?" Bailey asked.

"I don't see why not. It's for sale. There gonna be people going in and out of that house all the time until someone buys it." Clara Mae lowered her voice. "I don't know who is gonna want to buy it in the condition it's in. I don't know why Harriet don't want to fix it up."

"Maybe she doesn't have the money," Bailey suggested. "That might be why she's selling it now after all these years."

"You know... I didn't think of that," Clara Mae said. "But then again, she got enough to pay some lawyer to take care of the sale."

"Where is the law office located?" Bailey asked. It was possible Clara Mae wouldn't know the answer, but her daughter would.

"It's some big firm in New York."

Bailey smiled. "So, it's possible that Harriet lives there."

"That's what I'm thinking," Clara Mae said. "Figures she'd

go back up north. She was like her mama in that way— wanting to live all fancy. Harriet never liked living down here 'cause it was too country. Used to always say that she was going back to the big city when she grew up." Picking up her phone, she said, "I'll call Sharon to get that code for you."

"Thank you for all your help."

Bailey thought about her conversation with Kaile concerning Harini. *I still can't connect the two of them together. Maybe Trace is right about this—I'm just pulling at straws.*

She decided to follow through on seeing the house since Clara Mae went to the trouble of getting the code for her. Bailey decided she would spend the night and head back home in the morning. She was disappointed over having wasted time and money traveling back and forth to Georgia.

BAILEY PARKED in front of what was once the Spook family home.

There was a mediocre attempt at landscaping: fresh mulch, parched fall mums, and a worn welcome mat. Okay, not every house sparkled with curb appeal, Bailey decided. And Clara Mae did mention that the home was in a poor condition.

She punched in the code she'd been given into the lockbox.

The key popped out and she inserted it, forcing a sticky deadbolt open.

Inside the tiny foyer, the rancid stale aroma of a house which had been empty for years assailed her. Bailey inhaled deeply, quickly ruling out the smell of rotting wood.

She hoped to get a real feel for Randy Spook and his life here in this house. The soft muted yellow hues in the wallpaper was not too feminine. The wrought iron lighting fixtures were nice and most likely considered elegant and upscale years ago.

She chose to venture up the short flight of stairs first, then work her way back down.

Alternating between her camera and typing notes on her iPad, Bailey took photographs and jotted down the obvious in the closet size bedroom designated as the master: a queen-sized bed with a wooden headboard, hardwood floors, windows draped with dark burgundy curtains. No blinds.

She walked into the bedroom across the hall. In contrast, it was decorated in a soft lavender and sage theme. This was probably Harriet's room, Bailey decided. The third bedroom was decorated in a blue and white theme. The wallpaper was dotted with footballs. Randy's room she surmised. The three bedrooms shared a cornflower blue-tiled hall bath.

Downstairs, she navigated to the kitchen. It was a nice size, but smaller than Bailey had imagined. The pale-yellow walls were complemented by white appliances and cabinets.

"Ridiculously dated but clean if you clear all the years of dust," she murmured as she took pictures.

The living room showed off dusty drapes, heavy and mauve. "This was once a very nice home," Bailey murmured. A few pieces of furniture remained in the house covered with sheets.

She walked through the living room, checking out the furniture. Mrs. Spook had been a fan of Queen Anne styled furnishings.

Unless a realtor convinced a potential buyer there was buried treasure, they'd never sell this house as far as she was concerned.

Clara Mae had mentioned before Bailey left that she'd heard Dr. Spook intended on renovating the house but never got around to going through with it. She said she'd overheard the doctor and his wife arguing from time to time about starting the renovations.

Initially, Bailey had no desire to explore the basement area, but her gut refused to let her leave without doing so.

There was a decent size laundry room, which connected to an empty one-car garage. Her eyes traveled over to a door near the stairs.

Curious, Bailey decided to investigate.

She opened the door and stale air rushed past her as if on a mad dash for the exit.

Her curiosity paid off.

Inside was a couple of boxes covered with a thick coating of dust and cobwebs. Bailey debated whether or not to take them with her. It was pretty clear by the thick layer of dust that no one knew they were in the closet and had been for years.

She decided to take them with her. Bailey vowed that she would give them to Harriet once she found her.

Back at the hotel, she settled down and opened the first box, which was filled with family photos and mementos.

Bailey found copies of the birth certificates. There were several photographs of the family; although most of them during their childhood. She saw an envelope and picked it up. Bailey was surprised to see it contained original manuscripts of his published work. There were also a couple of what appeared to be completed drafts.

Her fingertips flew over the words as if it were braille. Pressing the pages hard between her hand and lap, Bailey stopped reading and stared at the manuscript, her emotions equally mixed. There was a part of her that wished she hadn't read it, but more so, she was wildly tempted to reveal what she'd discovered.

She spent the next hour on her laptop, going through image after image of Harini; hoping to catch a glimpse of a bare left arm. Bailey needed to see if there was a birthmark.

Finally, she found a photograph of Harini in a strapless dress.

The birthmark was just as Clara Mae described.

Bailey placed a hand to her mouth. Could it be?

Could she really be Harriet Spook? If so, Harini Samuels was a complete fraud.

Bailey broke into a grin. "I've got you now." She knew there was more to Harini's relationship with Randy because of how hard she'd worked to cover up her identity. "That's why you hired the lawyer. You don't want people to know the truth about you. You stole your brother's work and published it as your own."

Another thought entered her mind. How did Pip fit into this puzzle?

BAILEY WALKED INTO THE HOUSE. "Trace, where are you?"

"In the office," he responded.

"Hey honey."

"I didn't expect you home until Sunday." He got up and walked around the desk. "I'm glad you're here. I missed you."

Bailey kissed him. "I've got good news. I found the connection between Harini and Randy. I found copies of his manuscripts—she published them as her own."

"So, what do you plan to do with the information?" Trace asked.

"I haven't decided yet." Bailey took a seat. "Honey, I watched a documentary last night on narcissistic personality disorder. It caught my attention because when they were talking about the symptoms—I thought of Harini. According to the documentary, people with this mental condition have an inflated sense of their own importance, a desperate need for excessive attention and admiration, and they lack empathy for others. Harini definitely loves attention, and she has an exaggerated sense of her own importance. According to her—she's the greatest at everything. She once told me that she was the best writer she knew…" Bailey chuckled. "I couldn't believe she really said that."

"Honey, the cornerstone of narcissism is lack of empathy. People with this disorder do not see or realize the impact their behavior has on others. They don't step into someone else's shoes. They see only their needs. Their sense of entitlement is paramount. Beneath is low self-esteem. They have trouble keeping friends, are basically unhappy when they don't receive the admiration they believe they deserve."

"I know for a fact that she's exaggerated some of her *accomplishments*. Anybody with the Internet can verify things like awards, sales, bestseller lists…" Bailey paused a moment then said, "But now I get why she only associates with certain authors—it's because she thinks she's superior and she considers them her equal. Everyone else is inferior."

Trace nodded in agreement. "Could be."

"So, taking advantage of others to get what she wants, being arrogant and pretentious… all of this is because of her disorder?"

"Yes."

"So, she's not being malicious then," Bailey said. "Harini simply can't help herself. In her mind, she believes that everyone is envious of her, when in truth—Harini's the one who's envious."

"You maybe right about this."

"I feel bad for her, but I still need to confront her," Bailey said. "She needs someone to call her out on her mess. What's she's done has hurt other authors—some who aren't going to write anymore. If it hadn't been for you, Trace… I don't know if I'd even be published right now." She paused a moment, then said, "I need to go to Philadelphia. This is not about revenge anymore. I can't let her do this to one more person. I have to try and stop her."

"I'll go with you."

Bailey shook her head no. "I need to do this alone. I'm flying out on Sunday evening."

Chapter 26

The organist had begun the prelude by the time Harini walked into the sanctuary. Her nose was assaulted by the startling clash of women's perfume and men's cologne which almost over-powered the musty odor of hymnals.

A smiling usher in a dark suit led her down the center aisle to the fourth row. Her face impassive, Harini groaned inwardly. She preferred to sit toward the rear, where she could blend into anonymity.

She sat in a pew, captivated by the words of a hymn she could not identify. Eyes closed, Harini felt the firmness of the pew beneath her bottom.

Coming here made Harini feel at peace. The church, she believed, was a place where forgiveness could be granted by showing up. She opened her eyes for a moment, her gaze trav-eled the room. People in the congregation were deep in prayer —something she'd given up on years ago.

Prayers were meant to be answered. So far, Harini's had not been. She was alone—no husband or even a suitable prospect. She couldn't carry a baby to term.

Her eyes remained shut as her mind absorbed the fading

tendrils of solitude. Harini heard the heavy creak of the vestibule doors and felt sunlight spread across her back. It penetrated, refreshing her.

In her mind, Harini could see her mother dressed in a green robe seated in the choir. Her mother loved to sing. She loved the attention.

Pip shared their mother's gift while Harini couldn't carry a tune if she tried. She was forced to sit back and watch as others adored her mother and brother's talent. She often fantasized of being on stage with millions of fans in the audience. Her mind drifted to when she was seven years old and she wanted to be Snow White in the school play. She wanted it so badly that she'd harassed little Stephanie Myers into quitting. She'd practiced every single day and knew the part, but when the curtains opened—she stood there frozen. Her parents were furious.

In high school, she ruined her competition's reputation by telling everyone that the girl was nothing more than a slut. Harini had even started a rumor that the girl was pregnant. It didn't matter because she was the better choice for the cheer-leading captain. Under her leadership the squad won numerous awards. However, it was not enough to please her mother and father. Cheerleading was not a prestigious sport. Not like football and Pip's role as quarterback. Even when he stopped playing the sport—they did not see it as failure on his part.

Harini never finished college, although she'd listed both an undergrad and graduate degree in her author biography. It was a harmless lie, she told herself. Millions of people have lied about their educational achievements. It didn't mean they didn't possess the knowledge.

I'm very intelligent—have always been smart. Even my mother used to tell me all the time that I was much too smart for my own good.

Harini wrapped her arms tight around herself, crossing the sleeves of her bright teal shirt. Her right hand rose up her arm and she felt the birthmark. It was a symbol of self-preservation and instinct.

"How was church?" Pip inquired when she arrived home an hour and a half later.

"You could've come with me."

"Why would I do that?"

Harini rolled her eyes at her brother. "You can be so spiteful at times."

"I have reason to be."

"All I want is to have a nice peaceful afternoon. Can I have that please? I need to get some writing done."

"Write away."

"Pip…"

Harini released a long sigh. She hated when her brother got into one of his moods. She wanted to toss some ideas around with him, but when Pip was like this—it was fruitless. She wouldn't see him for the rest of the day.

"YOU'RE sure you want to do this?" Trace asked when they pulled in front of RDU Airport. "A woman like this could be dangerous."

Bailey nodded. "I have to do it. It's time Harini and I had it out. I'm not afraid of her, honey. She isn't going to attack me, especially not face to face. She'd be more worried that someone will capture it on video."

"I don't know about this. Maybe I should go with you."

"Honey, you don't have to come," she assured him. "I'll be fine. Besides, I have my taser right here." Bailey patted her purse. "I keep it with me."

Trace didn't look convinced.

"All I want to do is talk to Harini. I can't allow her to continue to hurt other people. She's gotten away with this for too long. I just want to make her understand that this has to end."

"And if she doesn't agree? What then? Are you prepared to take this to the finish line?"

"Yes," Bailey responded. "I will make sure the entire world knows what she did."

"What I can't figure out is how Pip fits into all this?" Trace said. "You said that you saw the birth certificates."

"I'm confused as well," she said. "Maybe her father had an outside child. Miss Clara Mae did hint that he was a bit of a womanizer. Then again, maybe Harini just calls him her brother. I feel like Maurie and Cassidy are more like my sisters than my own are."

Concern colored his expression. "I want you to be careful, Bailey."

"Trace, I'm going to be fine," she assured him.

"Call me before and after you meet with that woman."

"I will."

"I mean it, Bailey. I want to know that you're okay," Trace said. "If I don't hear from you—I'm coming up there."

———

BAILEY FLEW TO PHILADELPHIA.

Maurie and Cassidy picked her up from the airport when the plane landed.

"My girls…"

"It's so good to see you," Maurie said after giving Bailey a hug.

She embraced Cassidy next. "I'm so happy to see y'all."

Bailey placed her overnight tote in the back of Maurie's SUV, then opened the rear passenger door and climbed inside.

"I can't believe you are here to confront Harini," Cassidy said. "Is it really worth it?"

"I think so," Bailey responded. "I'm doing this because she's hurting other authors, Cass. This can't continue."

"What exactly do you have on this woman?"

"Randy Spook is her brother," Bailey announced. "I have proof that she took his work and published it as her own."

Maurie gasped. "Are you serious? I've read his books and I never would've put the two of them together. Are you sure about this?"

"I have two of his manuscripts complete with his notes on the projects. They are the first two books Harini released. Everything including the changes he made are in her books."

"I'm not surprised," Cassidy said. "I told you she was fake."

"It's terrible that Harini could do something like that to her own brother," Maurie interjected.

"Exactly," Bailey responded. "So, you know she doesn't care about anybody else. I'm picking up a rental in the morning and I'm going to see her tomorrow."

"What do you expect to accomplish?" Cassidy asked.

"I'm going to make it clear to Harini that her reign of terror is going to end, or I will put her on blast. I'll expose the one secret she thought was dead and buried to the world."

Cassidy turned in her seat to face Bailey. "Be careful. That woman is a sociopath as far as I'm concerned."

"I'll be fine. Harini isn't going to want the truth to come out. It will ruin her."

"Is she expecting you?"

"Cass, I thought about calling her, but then I decided it was best to just show up. I don't want to give her any kind of heads up. I'm going to blindside Harini the same way she did me."

"Sounds like you're still wanting some payback, Bailey."

"I don't deny that, Maurie. I'm looking forward to getting even with Harini once and for all. Trace thinks that she has a narcissistic personality disorder and he could be right, but I don't care. She still needs to be confronted with the truth, then maybe she'll go sit down somewhere." Bailey stared out the window. "I can't wait to get a cheesesteak and a tuna hoagie. I've missed them so much." She was done with having to provide reasons for wanting to confront Harini—the woman didn't deserve any sympathy from Bailey. And she would get none.

THE NEXT MORNING, Bailey picked up her rental, then headed out to the Washington Square West area.

Just as she opened the vehicle door, Bailey glimpsed Harini's shiny black Mercedes exiting the parking garage. She slammed her door and started the car.

She caught up with Harini at the stop light a block away. Bailey didn't care where she was going—she was determined to have her say.

"I told you one day I would make you pay. That day has come, Harini Samuels."

Bailey meant it when she said she had forgiven Harini, but it didn't mean she would just stand by and let the woman continue hurting other authors.

"What in the world…" she whispered.

Bailey pulled the car into the parking lot across the street from the Grant Memorial Garden Cemetery.

This setting was not what Bailey had in mind, but she was determined to follow through with her plan. She eased out of the vehicle slowly.

Maybe she's visiting Randy's grave, Bailey considered. She decided to give Harini some time alone.

Her cell phone rang.

It was Cassidy.

She let the call go to voicemail.

Bailey stepped out of the rental, locking the doors behind her.

It was time to have that face to face with Harini.

Her eyes traveled her surroundings, searching for one person in particular. Bailey walked up a grassy knoll, staying close to the path. She spied a gathering of people a few yards away. She knew they were laying a loved one to rest.

She walked faster.

Bailey heard Harini's voice before she spotted her beneath a huge tree.

"You can be so insensitive at times," she heard Harini say. "Why can't you have my back on this?"

Bailey watched in disbelief a moment before asking, "Who are you talking to?"

Harini turned around, a look of complete shock on her face. "What are you doing here? A cemetery is supposed to be a place where people find comfort among their friends, family and ancestors. How dare you interrupt a private moment."

"*Who were you talking to?*" Bailey asked a second time as her eyes traveled their surroundings. "'Cause there's nobody here but you and me."

Harini looked confused for a moment before responding, "People talk to their loved ones all the time—those who have gone too soon."

Bailey glanced down at the name on the tombstone.

Randall James Spook
(Pip)
Beloved brother
1980 to 2004

"Why are you *here*?" Harini demanded.

"I came to talk to you. You were leaving when I got to your place, so I followed you here."

"We have nothing to discuss."

"Oh, we have a lot to talk about, Harini," Bailey said. She glanced back down at the tombstone. "*A lot.* I saw Colton a few months back when I was in Texas. We had a very interesting conversation about you." She met Harini's hard gaze. "He mentioned meeting Pip."

"And?"

"Well, that's not possible," Bailey responded as she pointed to the tombstone. "What did you do? Hire someone to play your brother so he wouldn't find out the truth."

Harini did not respond.

"You know you're really something else. You've spent your whole career doing every underhanded thing possible to be number one in this industry. You've blackmailed, manipulated, straight lied on and stolen ideas from the very people who looked up to you." Bailey paused a moment before continuing. "Including your own *brother*."

Harini paled. "Excuse me? I was very close to my brother. I gave him that nickname. Our parents hated it. When nobody was around, I called him Pip." She broke into a rare tender smile. "Sis was his term of endearment for me."

"This is all very sweet, but the fact is that you stole your brother's manuscript and published it as your own. Did Pip find out before he died? Did he confront you about it?"

"You have no idea what you're talking about."

"Oh, I think I do," Bailey countered. "You went behind Pip's back and submitted his manuscript. I read your first two books, so you can imagine my surprise when I found the original manuscripts with your brother's name on them."

"Girl, you talking crazy."

"I'm not the one who's crazy," Bailey countered. "You're the one who's been living with your dead brother all these years. I can only assume it's because you feel guilty over what you did to him. That's why you can't let him go—why you moved his grave to Philadelphia. You left your parents buried in Georgia."

"See," Pip said, "I told you that she was the wrong one to mess with, but you wouldn't listen. I told you someone would one day discover the truth of what happened."

"Shut up," Harini uttered. She turned to face her brother. "Pip, this witch can't prove nothing, so keep your mouth shut."

Bailey eyed the woman deeply involved in a conversation with a ghost. Her anger and thirst for vengeance melted into pity for a woman so haunted by the sins of her past.

"Harini, you need help."

"I don't need anything," she snapped in response. A cold look came into Harini's eyes, making them almost black. "You're nothing, Bailey Hargrove. *Nothing*. You can go around trying to spread your lies about me but nobody's gonna believe you."

"They're not lies, Harini," Bailey stated. "I have proof. I know who and what you really are, *Harriet Spook*. You and I both know the truth. She pointed to Harini's arm. "That birthmark on your arm is very fitting because you're toxic... just pure poison."

"You don't know anything," Harini hissed. "My brother had everything. I deserved something good to come my way. I wanted to be a writer. Pip didn't even like to read... but he writes two books and the world considers them masterpieces. The manuscript I submitted kept getting rejected... Pip was in the hospital. Father kept saying that he wasn't gonna make it... He was dying."

"*He was your brother*."

"He was gonna die. They would've just sat there gathering dust." Her arms folded across her chest, Harini asked, "So, what happens now?"

"I haven't quite decided," Bailey confessed. "Seeing you

239

like this... talking to a ghost... I'm beginning to think that's punishment enough."

"I haven't committed any crime," Harini said. "I don't understand why you *wanna be* authors don't get that there are only a few plots in this world. We can both have the same idea but come up with different stories."

"It is astounding that you actually believe this is okay," Bailey said. "It's one thing to come up with a similar concept but you *steal* from other writers. Then you threaten to expose their secrets to keep them from putting you on blast. You want them to believe that you have power—that you can ruin careers, but in reality, you're powerless. You are nothing more than an insecure woman who is slowly losing her mind."

Harini glanced over at Pip. "You're not gonna say anything? You're just going to let her talk to me like this?"

He gave a slight shrug. "It's time you heard the truth, sis."

"I feel sorry for you." Bailey switched her purse from one side to the other. "I pray one day you'll get the help you so desperately need." She paused a moment before continuing. "I could go public with what I know and ruin your life, but then I'd be no better than you. I don't want to leave behind a legacy of poison—there are already too many poison pens in this world. It's a shame that people like you aren't smart enough to recognize that there is room for all of us in this industry. It's sad that you don't have enough faith in your own writing."

An evil grin spread across Harini's face. "I *want* you to take me to court. Just do it. I'll be here long after everyone forgets about you," she responded. "You're gifted, but you're weak—that's why you won't last in this business. I will always be better than you."

Bailey laughed. "I'll believe that when you come up with an actual story idea on your own—not something you've stolen from someone else. Be original for once... be organic..."

"Where are my brother's manuscripts? That stuff belongs to me. I can have you charged with theft."

"Don't tell her," Pip said.

"Stay out of this," Harini warned her brother.

"They're in a safe place," Bailey responded as if she'd heard him. "From this point forward, you should either retire or find a way to come up with your own storylines. Make an announcement that you are no longer mentoring other writers —you can say that you need to focus on your own work."

"Bravo...," Pip said. "If I were you, I'd do what she suggests, sis."

Harini glared at her brother, before turning to face Bailey. "When I get through with you, nobody will ever—"

She interrupted Harini by saying, "If I hear of you hurting another author, I promise I'll make sure the world knows that your first two books were written by Randy. This ends now. One more thing, Harini," Bailey said. "I forgive you for everything you've done to me. Hopefully one day you'll be able to forgive yourself."

"Humph... I sleep every night," she retorted.

"But you live with a ghost every day. I've said everything I needed to say. And I mean every word of it. Do as I asked or face the consequences."

Bailey glanced down at the grave and whispered, "Rest in Heaven, Randy. From everything I've read and heard about you—you were too good for this world."

She turned to leave.

Without looking back, Bailey said, "Goodbye Harini."

Chapter 27

"That spiteful little witch think she's gotten the best of me," Harini huffed. She bent down to pick up a nearby rock lying in front of a crumbling headstone. "I'm going to beat her brains out."

"Don't do it, sis," Pip warned.

"I want those manuscripts. I'm not gonna let Bailey hold anything over my head. If I have to involve the police to get them—I will."

Harini was practically running now along the cracked cement pathway, trying to catch up with Bailey. "No one is gonna blackmail me."

Not paying attention to where she was walking, Harini tripped over a large discolored stone and was unable to break her fall.

On the way down, she struck her head on a tombstone. A piece of broken glass cutting a deep gash, severing the Jugular vein.

Blackness surrounded her.

WHEN SHE OPENED HER EYES, Harini found Pip beside her, her hand in his. "I can feel your touch," she murmured as she sat up.

Harini touched her forehead. "I fell."

Pip nodded. "You did. You were going after Bailey."

She rose to her feet. "I've got to stop her."

"Sis, it's too late."

"No, I need to get those manuscripts from her. Pip, you know they belong to me."

Harini suddenly felt strange... like she was a bit disoriented. It was then she noticed the woman lying on the ground, blood seeping from the ugly gash on her forehead. "That's me," she murmured.

"It was a bad fall."

"I'm..." Stunned, Harini shook her head in denial. "Nooo..."

"Sis, you're dead. Like me."

"But, I don't want to be—there was still so much I wanted to do with my life." Harini glanced around. "That's why I could feel your touch."

She looked at him. "You didn't leave me..."

Harini thought back to the day her brother died. He'd only been home from the hospital a few hours. She wanted to try and make him understand why she'd submitted his work as her own—how badly she needed to be published—it had been her dream. He wanted nothing to do with her. Pip refused to talk to her.

"You're thinking about that day."

"Pip, I just wanted to talk, but you were so mean to me. You said you were going to tell our parents what I'd done. I ran off when you collapsed. I wanted to save you, but I panicked."

"We see that day differently," he responded. "What I remember is that you wanted to save yourself more. You just stood there and watched me die. You didn't call out for the nurse… I saw it in your eyes. You wanted me dead."

"I just wanted to be number one, Pip."

The October weather was cool, and the wind was howling, the eerie sound bouncing off the tombstones, some centuries old, and others like the one nearby, erected a few days ago.

All around, fearless magnolia trees stood sentry over the graves as the wind whistled through fresh cut grass.

Across the grounds a stream of cars including a black hearse were parked at the curb, while black-clad mourners sat beneath a tent to say final goodbyes. Some of them could be heard crying while one after the other laid flowers atop the coffin.

The headstone closest to them felt cold to the touch.

Harini felt a whoosh of air penetrate her body. "I never thought we would end up here in such a cold, dark place."

This would now become her eternal home.

"How could you let this happen?" she asked Pip.

"This is all your fault. You just had to seek revenge. Why couldn't you just do the right thing for once?"

Harini responded, "I couldn't let her win."

"Look around you. We're in a cemetery. You call this *winning*?"

"What did you expect me to do?"

"To become a better person. After everything that's happened, you haven't learned anything. Now it's too late."

"What do you mean that it's too late?"

Silence.

"Tell me," Harini insisted.

"You're dead, sis. There are no do overs. No more chances to do right by people. My life ended, but I was determined to make sure my death, though tragic, had a greater purpose. To get you to make better choices in your life."

"So, what happens next?" Harini asked.

"*Judgement Day*," Pip answered before fading from view.

"WOW, I CAN'T BELIEVE IT," Bailey murmured as they walked out of the church. "Harini Samuels is dead."

"C'mon, you can tell me," Kaile said in a low whisper. "Did you kill her? They found her in the cemetery. That's where you confronted her, right?"

"I never touched her," Bailey responded with a chuckle. "I promise. I have no idea what happened after I left. Who knows? Maybe Pip did it."

They laughed.

"The flowers Lanelle sent were beautiful," Kaile said. "I can understand why she didn't want to come to the funeral. She has no love for Harini."

"I don't either," Bailey confessed. "But I felt I needed to come pay my respects."

"Well, I hate that she died. As far as I'm concerned, she got off way too easy." Kaile glanced over at the black hearse that would transport Harini's coffin to the cemetery.

"You really think so?" Bailey asked. "Her life has ended. Harini lived for the very attention that her death is receiving. It would've made her day to hear the words of adoration from her fans across the country. Her book sales are probably going to jump—everything that she's always wanted. But eventually, Harini's books will disappear from the shelves and she will become a distant memory. To her, that would be a fate worse than death."

"You're probably right," Kaile agreed. "One thing for sure... she would've loved her funeral. Her agent certainly did right by her. I heard that Harini's money will go to the American Heart Foundation in honor of her brother."

246

"That's a very generous gesture. I'm sure Pip would be pleased."

"Despite everything that she did—I really hope she and Pip can now rest in peace," Kaile said. "Before Harini showed me who she really was—I thought she was smart and so beautiful. I had no idea that she needed help mentally."

"There's no way you really could've known," Trace interjected. "People with narcissistic personality disorder don't cogitate that anything is wrong with them, so they're generally not going to seek treatment."

A fierce wind came through, chilling the air and whipping around them.

Kaile stopped in her tracks. "I'm not one for believing in ghosts, but do you think... 'cause I can't have this woman haunting me."

Bailey and Trace looked at one another, then burst into laughter.

"It's just windy out here," she reassured Kaile. "Are you going to the cemetery?"

"Yes. I want to make sure she's buried. I want to watch them throw the dirt into that hole."

"Trace and I need to head to the airport. Our flight leaves in a couple of hours." Bailey gave Kaile a hug. "It's always good seeing you."

Later in the rental vehicle, Bailey asked, "Trace, do you believe that Harini could really see her brother—in the same way I'm looking right at you?"

"I believe that a spirit's connection with the living provides a certain solace—it can ease the pain of the loss for some people."

"I suppose that's a good thing."

Trace wrapped an arm around Bailey. "I'm glad we can finally put this experience with Harini behind us."

"Me, too," she responded. "I feel better knowing that she's

no longer preying on writers who only want to see their books on the shelves. The world needs all of our stories.

There's no need for competition."

"Unfortunately, there will always be Harini Samuels' in the world," Trace said. "They will never cease to exist."

"And there will always be someone who isn't afraid to speak up," responded Bailey.

"What are you planning to do with those manuscripts?"

"I thought about giving them to her agent since she's the executor of Harini's estate, but then she would know the truth which could've led to all kinds of legal issues. I gave them to the funeral director and requested that he put them in her coffin. Harini will literally take the truth of what happened between her and Pip to the grave."

"I guess that's the end of that story."

Grinning, Bailey shook her head. "Honey, you know me better than that. I'm not going to stoop to public shaming, but I am going to write a fictionalized version of what happened between Randy and Harini. I even have the perfect title for it… Poison Pen."

About the Author

 Jacquelin Thomas is an award winning, bestselling author with 80 titles in print and twenty-one years' experience as a published author. Her books have garnered several awards, including two EMMA awards, the Romance in Color Reviewers Award, Readers' Choice Award and the Atlanta Choice Award in the Religious & Spiritual category.

Jacquelin was a 2005 honoree at the Houston Black Film Festival for the movie adaptation of her novel, Hidden Blessings. She received a Living Legacy Award in 2017, and a Lifetime Achievement Award from Romantic Times Magazine.

Jacquelin is published in the romance, women's fiction, inspirational and young adult genres. Her second book in the young adult series, Divine Confidential was nominated for a 2008 NAACP Image Award for outstanding fiction.

Jacquelin and her family live in North Carolina.

CPSIA information can be obtained
at www.ICGtesting.com
Printed in the USA
LVHW091844260219
608806LV00001B/96/P